# MASTER OF DRYFORD

Felicia found the strength to escape from her evil stepfather. But, without money or position, how could a single girl win the struggle to be independent in Victorian England? Then, a chance meeting with the debonair Charles brings Felicia to Dryford as governess. But the ancient family home is overshadowed by mystery, and she has to earn the trust of her new family before dramatic events reveal to her the whole truth — and her love for the Master of Dryford.

*Books by Helen Magee*

**FALSE ENCHANTMENT**

# HELEN MAGEE

# MASTER OF DRYFORD

## Complete and Unabridged

PIP
POLLINGER IN PRINT

Pollinger Limited
9 Staple Inn
Holborn
LONDON
WC1V 7QH

www.pollingerltd.com

First published in Great Britain under the name of Elinor Dean
First Edition published by Robert Hale 1984
This large print edition published by Pollinger in Print 2007

A CIP catalogue record is available from the British Library

ISBN 978-1-905665-36-5

For Aunt Mary,
with love

# 1

It was in the last rays of the setting sun that I first saw the keep from which Keep Dryford takes its name and I treasure the memory for I will never see it again. It was oddly comforting though a little frightening looming black and solid against the sky which flamed blood-red behind it and I felt at once a sense of peace at its timelessness and a thrill of fear at the violence it had seen in its time.

I was running away, escaping my past, and beside me stood the man who had made it possible. Behind me was fear but I did not think of that as I watched the sun slide from the sky and the dark outline of the Keep soften and merge into the dusk, or the gloaming as it is known here in Scotland. All I thought was that here was a new beginning, here I would be safe from threats and terror and fear but I could not have known how wrong I was. For me the fears were only just beginning. And perhaps that's where I should start — right at the very beginning . . .

\* \* \*

My childhood was a happy one. My parents, though not wealthy, were not poor either and I remember with affection the small Queen Anne house on the outskirts of London with its lawns sweeping down to the river. It was a long time before I was able to connect that much-loved stretch of water at the bottom of our garden with the majestic expanse of the Thames that I gazed at in awe on our infrequent visits to the great city. I remember the excitement of those visits. The great shops of Bond Street lit by gas jets and so splendid that they seemed like palaces to me, the stalls in the streets where in winter you could buy a bag of roasted chestnuts which warmed your hands as well as tasting strange and delicious. The flower-sellers in summer from whom Father would always buy a posy for Mother. The hiss of steam and the smell of the great railway station, the noise and clamour as the train pulled in seeming to my childish eyes like a huge dragon; and the journey home again, half-asleep with the wonder of it all and always, at the journey's end home, never changing, safe and comforting. It seemed to me then that nothing could ever change. There seemed always to be laughter in my life, my mother's sparkling like the river on a sunny day, my father's full-throated and deep like the dark river pools. I don't remember my father so very clearly now, only strong brown hands and laughing eyes as he swung me up in his arms and I seemed to touch the clouds or held me close to him when a childish nightmare disturbed my dreams. They called me Felicia which means happiness, and they taught me by their lives the meaning of the word.

My mother was devastated when he died. I remember she seemed to shrink a little as if without his energy and strength she somehow became less of a person. I was ten at the time and for the next year I watched as the mother I had known became more fragile, more vulnerable. Even the pretty colour seemed to drain out of her cheeks and it was not just that she was wearing black. It was more than that. Father had been her strength and she was quite simply lost without him. But even I did not realise the extent of her grief, not until a year after Father's death when she came out of mourning.

I was playing in the garden when Mrs Larkin came to fetch me.

'You're wanted in the small sitting room. Miss Felicia,' she said.

I looked up at her. Mrs Larkin was a small rotund woman who always seemed to breathe cheerfulness and good sense, but her face was almost grim as she spoke. She and her husband had looked after us as long as I could remember, she as cook housekeeper and he as gardener and odd-job man. I had never seen her look so stern.

'Why, what's the matter?' I said.

Her lips pursed up in a thin line as she said,

'That's not for me to say. Your Mama wants to see you so come along and don't go upsetting her, poor woman, as if she didn't have troubles enough.'

She went on in this vein as we walked towards the house but even the unusual severity of her manner did nothing to prepare me for what was to come.

Mother was sitting on the sofa when I entered the room,

'My darling, Felicia,' she said drawing me into her arms, 'I have some grave news.'

She looked up pleadingly at a tall thin man standing behind her. I had barely noticed him as I came into the room but I looked at him now and I did not like him. With all the stubborn prejudice of a child I hated him on sight. He looked down at her. His long thin face with its dead eyes and side whiskers made me shiver though I still stood within the circle of my mother's arms.

'The child must know, my dear,' he said. 'She is not an infant.'

I turned to my mother. There were tears on her long lashes and her mouth trembled as she spoke to me.

'My love, the house will have to be sold.' I was stunned. The house. My home. The only one I had ever known. The river at the edge of the lawns. The tree where Father had hung a swing for me, so long ago it seemed to me then. His study where I could still go and curl up in his chair and smell that familiar tobacco smell, where I could imagine I could hear his voice, his laugh. I clung to her. She was still speaking, explaining in words I could barely take in that we had no money. I was bewildered. Never before had either of my parents spoken to me of money. Never before had it even entered my head to think of it. I remember saying in wonder,

'Money?', as if it were a word in a foreign language, then he spoke again.

'The reason, my dear. The child must know the reason,' and for the first time I felt his cold eyes on me and shivered.

She looked up at him again and her voice was a whisper.

'No, you cannot. She is only a child.'

He bent over her and she seemed to shrink from him. 'If you do not then I will,' he said.

She ran her tongue over dry lips. The tears were flowing freely now. 'Your father,' she said, 'your dear father . . . '

5

'Leonora,' the voice was hard and she flinched.

'He left us very badly off,' she continued. 'There were debts that we cannot pay.' She faltered to a halt and held me to her. 'Oh, my darling, I am so sorry, so sorry.'

Then a hand gripped my arm. I looked at it as if it were some curious object in a museum. There were long black hairs on the back of it and underneath the skin was white and smooth. I looked up at the face so close to mine. There were hairs growing out of the nostrils and his lips were very full and very red. Behind them his teeth were long and pointed. Like a wolf, I thought, and suddenly into my mind came the thought of my father sitting me on his knee, his hands brown and square and his laughing eyes looking into mine as he told me the story of Red Riding Hood. He was speaking,

'Your father was a gambler, Felicia, a gambler, do you hear? He lost your house, your security, your future on the turn of a card. You have nothing now. Nothing but the clothes you wear. Everything else will have to be sold. Your father died a bankrupt,' he almost spat out the last word. The face came nearer, the teeth gleamed sharply and I thought, he's going to eat me up.

It was then that I began to scream. I kicked at his shins and tore myself away. I took one

6

last look at the hideous face and even my mother's arms could not stay me as I ran out of the house and down the garden to the hollow tree that had been my refuge in time of trouble — when a favourite doll was broken or a bird was found dead on the lawn. But this was worse than a broken doll or a dead bird. This was my home, my life, all I had known. I had not understood all he had been saying. I did not know what bankrupt meant but I had understood that my life as I had known it was over and I had under- stood that he had been telling me that my father was wicked and *that* I would never believe. He was the wicked one with his wolf's teeth and his cold eyes. I knew my fairy-tales. I knew that bad people always told lies about good people so I sat in my hiding place and I hated him with all my strength and as I rubbed the tears fiercely out of my eyes I wondered what his punishment would be for, child that I was, I still believed in fairytales.

If I was unhappy then, it was nothing to the waves of fear and loneliness that engulfed me when my mother eventually came to me. God knows how she had persuaded him to let her come alone, but she had. My eyes were dry. I had no more tears and she put her arms around me. Her face was white and her eyes huge with a fear that I know now was as great as mine.

'Felicia,' she said, 'there is one more thing you have to know.' I looked at her. I could feel nothing. Her voice trembled as she said it. 'That man. The man you have just met. His name is Mr Petheridge and I am going to marry him.'

That was the end of my childhood. I was eleven years old when I grew up. Mr Petheridge was a good man, my mother said. He had helped her through the last year, paid our household bills, settled outstanding debts. She was greatly indebted to him. He did good works among the poor. He was a lay preacher with a small private income. She told me these things with a pale set face and I understood. She needed someone to look after her. She was a widow with no money, no home and a child to care for. It seemed to me later that I did all my growing up in that single afternoon while the bees hummed lazily in the long grass by the water's edge and inside I was still screaming for my father.

So we left our beautiful home and went to live with Mr Petheridge in an ugly red brick house in London where Mr Petheridge ran our lives with a rod of iron and his sour-faced sister kept house. She had iron grey hair scraped back into a bun and her face was mottled. I never saw her smile. For three years I watched my mother fade and wither until she died, from despair I suppose, and I was left alone in an ugly house with ugly people. I was fourteen and I knew that he had killed my mother. He had bought her and he had killed her.

When she died my formal education stopped. I had always been 'good at my books' as Mrs Larkin used to put it and I found out very quickly that this talent for learning was a valuable weapon in my armoury against my stepfather. I was sent to a dingy day school for the 'daughters of gentlefolk' from which I would have emerged as ignorant as I arrived had it not been for him. He took great delight in setting me tests of knowledge and his scorn was poured unceasingly on me when I failed to meet the impossibly-high standard he set for me. It was not long before I realised that he did this to torture my mother who could not bear to see my misery at his taunts. Fragile though she was, she had a spirit that evaded him and that he knew he could never possess. So I scoured the meagre shelves of the school for books and tormented my inadequate teachers with my thirst for knowledge, spending long hours in my room poring over books when I should have been asleep until he could no longer reduce me to quivering inadequacy with his slights and between us grew up a hatred so strong that it frightened me with its intensity.

Even now I can hardly bear to think of the next four years, the years that followed my mother's death. I helped Miss Petheridge in the house, eking out the meagre allowance my stepfather made; I wore my hair scraped back from my face and secured it as best I could in the unbecoming bun that he insisted on. It was a major source of contention with him, my hair, for I had inherited my looks from my father and it sprang away from my face in a torrent of dark waves. I used to sit by the light of my candle at night and let it fall over my shoulders and brush it. It was my best feature, that and the eyes that would become liquid as I thought of the happiness I had once enjoyed and would grow stormy and cold as I thought of my poor mother's last years. But during the day my hair was scraped back and I went in fear lest a single strand should escape for I would be accused of shameful vanity and worse and my stepfather would mouth at me until I shook from the violence of it. I had learned to shut my ears to what he said but his eyes hypnotised me as a snake does a rabbit. The hairstyle suited me well enough for I had nothing to recommend me. I was too thin and my face was pale and pinched and the clothes I wore, of heavy dark material, did nothing to enhance my appearance.

I used to slip out as often as I could to see the Larkins. They had been dismissed of course when Mother married Mr Petheridge but they too had come to London. Mr Larkin had got a job as manager of a small private hotel not far from where we lived, due more to Mrs Larkin's excellent cooking than to his managerial skills. Whilst mother was alive they had kept in touch by letter for their few attempts to visit her had been sharply discouraged by my stepfather. I had got into the habit of slipping round there on my way home from school when I knew my stepfather would be late home but now that I had left school it was becoming increasingly difficult to avoid him. Mrs Larkin always made us a pot of tea and gave me hot buttered muffins, shaking her head over how thin I had become.

'It's feeding up you want, Miss Felicia,' she would say and, one day, her head on one side and sympathy in her eyes, 'Such a pretty girl and such a waste. Still he's a good man, I suppose. It's the Lord's work he does.'

Mr Larkin guffawed, 'Lord's work!'

'Hush now, Larkin, she's only a child,' chided Mrs Larkin.

At the time I wondered what Mr Larkin meant. I know now. They were the only ones who showed me sympathy and even a little laughter during those long years and

I looked forward to the visits I managed to pay them.

It was when I was sixteen that I was told I had to help my stepfather in his work. I knew he worked among the poor of the city but the nature of the work he did was uncertain. I saw a different London then — a London filled with poverty and want, so different from the pretty city I had known with my parents and yet there was beauty there too in some measure. The people he went amongst, dispensing food and lectures, for the most part gave not a fig for him or for me either. We were looked on with mistrust, the things we brought taken from necessity. I would grow hot with embarrassment as I stood behind him while he lectured some poor woman, her children clinging to her skirts in fear of his voice, on the value of thrift and honesty. He would never give them money.

'Money,' he would say to me, 'is only a temptation to them. They spend it on drink while their children go hungry and barefoot or worse still,' and he leaned towards me, 'they gamble, and you know what that leads to, do you not, Felicia?'

It was a perpetual theme with him. Gambling was the greatest sin, the worst kind of evil and he never let me forget what my father's gambling had done to us.

He was right in a way, of course. As I grew older I began to understand more about my father. I remembered the evenings he would come home lit up as if from inside with a glow that would warm us all and there would be a celebration, a special treat — a new hat for Mother or a pretty frock for me. There would also be the evenings he arrived back, his step leaden and all the light gone from his eyes and sometimes, just occasionally, a piece of silver or a particularly nice china figurine would disappear from my mother's collection. I asked her about it once when I noticed that one of her favourite pieces had gone.

'Oh, I never really liked that figurine so very much and your father's business needs a little extra just at the moment.'

But I knew she had loved it and that it had been a very valuable piece. Oddly enough I never knew what my father's 'business' was. I suspect there was none. Even my stepfather never enlightened me about that, only about the horrors of gambling. If he was trying to make me hate gambling as he did then he did not succeed. If anything it made me more sympathetic towards the gambler for I also understood by then that a gambler is as incapable of stopping as the world is from turning and if I had to choose between my dear adorable laughing father and this creature of evil who was supposed to be so good then I welcomed the gambling.

It was not until the night of my eighteenth birthday that I realised just how evil he was. I was sitting by the light of my candle brushing my hair and wondering what the future held for me. It was so bleak all of a sudden that I laid my head on my arms and began to cry, not for the future but for the fact that my eighteenth birthday had gone unnoticed in that house. The tears welled-up and spilled over and my sobs prevented me from hearing the door open. It was not until a hand was laid on my shoulder that I realised I was not alone. I turned my head and saw it lying there, pale and smooth with black hairs so close that my breath disturbed them. I could feel the clammy sweat of the hand through the thin cotton of my nightgown and I was afraid. I looked up and I would have screamed but the breath caught in my throat as I saw his face. It leered at me and the eyes glittered in the dim light. I saw it move even closer to me, the lips parting, and there were those long pointed teeth, only this time I did not think — 'he is going to eat me up' — as I had done when a child. I knew what it was he wanted even before he said.

'You're eighteen now, Felicia. Not a child any more.'

His eyes were on mine, hypnotising me as they had always done but I felt strangely removed from the scene.

Into my mind came the picture of the poor women he helped and of one in particular. She could not have been any older than me and she stood there before him in her grim hovel, a younger brother and sister pale from hunger clinging to her tattered skirt as he pressed money into her hands and said,

'I will return later this evening to see that the money is well spent.'

I had stood there, uncomprehending, thinking only that he never gave them money but the girl's face rose once again before my eyes and I knew now that she had understood though I had not. I felt sick with disgust then another thought blotted out everything else and I said,

'Oh, my poor mother.'

It was as if I had struck him. His eyes were black, his skin livid and the ugly red lips curled back from those sharp teeth. His hands came up and wound themselves around my throat like great white snakes, his face was no more than an inch from mine. My mind snapped back and I opened my mouth to scream for help when a voice sounded like a whiplash in the room,

'Stop it.'

His eyes lost their glazed look and his hands slid from around my throat. I could not move. He turned aside and in the doorway I saw Miss Petheridge. She looked so comical in her calico nightgown, her hair in a plait down her back, that I wondered why I was not laughing.

'Go back to bed,' she said to her brother.

That was all but she said it in a voice like iron. He looked at her for a moment and went without a word. I turned to Miss Petheridge. She was looking closely at me and for the first time I saw sympathy in her eyes, then she too turned and left me without a word. She was right. There was nothing to say. I knew what I had to do. I sat huddled on the bed and waited. As soon as dawn began to break over the city I got up and packed my belongings into a valise, then I crept downstairs and out of the silent house. I had only one place to go and I went there.

Mrs Larkin was shocked to see me so early. She bustled about making tea.

'My dear, you look so ill. What can have happened?' I couldn't tell her of course so I merely said,

'I'm sorry, Mrs Larkin but I couldn't stay there any longer and I had nowhere else to go.' I added inconsequentially, 'I'm eighteen now.'

She looked long and hard at me, then said,

'Quite right, my dear. It's no life for a young girl living with two dry old sticks like that and not even related so to speak. You just get your breakfast down you and into bed. You look as if you haven't slept for a week.'

My lips were dry as I said, 'What if he comes looking for me?'

Mr Larkin drew himself up. He looked so big and kind and comfortable.

'Just let him try, my dear. Don't you worry about that.'

I felt safe again and it was lovely to be tucked up in a warm bed with a hot brick wrapped in flannel at my feet and Mrs Larkin's smiling face nodding at me.

He did come for me that week but I didn't see him. Mr Larkin dealt with him. I overheard their conversation later outside my room when they thought I was asleep.

'Threatened to get the police, he did,' said Mr Larkin indignantly, 'Police, I said. It's me that'll be getting the police to you and no mistake about it if I see you round here again.'

Mrs Larkin drew in her breath. 'What did he say to that?'

Mr Larkin's voice was gruff.

'Made some threats about hotel managers having to be respectable and a word in the right ear could put us on the streets . . . '

17

I heard Mrs Larkin give a sharp cry then Mr Larkin again,

'Now don't you worry yourself m'dear. I just told him that his sister wouldn't be too pleased to know he'd been round here and he went off with his tail between his legs. From what young Miss Felicia has said over the years I had a notion that would do the trick and it did. Seems she's the only one that can keep him in hand.'

I heard them go off down the stairs, Mr Larkin's voice still comforting and I lay there and wondered if I had done the right thing in coming to them or if I would just bring them trouble. And what did he mean 'respectable'? There was no more respectable couple in the world than the Larkins. As the weeks passed, however, and there was no sign of my stepfather I soon forgot the incident and set myself the task of making myself useful to the Larkins.

The next year was like an awakening for me. I had a good head for figures so not only did I help Mrs Larkin in the kitchen and in the hotel but I also got Mr Larkin's books in order.

'Well, my dear,' he said to me one day, 'with your head for business we might even make this place pay.'

I laughed for I knew the place paid quite well but the books had indeed been in a terrible state and I had been useful. It was an odd place, their little hotel. The guests were mostly business-men from other parts of the country who liked the homely atmosphere and the good food that came out of Mrs Larkin's kitchen and of course it had an added attraction. I don't know when I first discovered it but Mrs Larkin broached the subject one day as we were hulling strawberries.

'The little room at the back, my dear,' she said tentatively.

'I know it,' I said and suddenly I heard myself adding, 'It's a gaming room, isn't it?'

She flushed a little and looked embarrassed, but there was a twinkle in her eye.

'I didn't think you'd realised.'

'I only just have, Mrs Larkin, and to think that all this time I've been living in a gambling den, a place of vice and immorality.'

She looked up at me and twinkled again as she saw that I was laughing.

'There now, and who'd have thought that you'd be able to laugh about that. You surely are improving, my dear, and looking very pretty if I may say so since you stopped scraping your hair back in that silly old bun.'

I laughed again and caught sight of myself in the mirror over the dresser. I did look almost pretty with my usually pale cheeks flushed from the heat of the kitchen and my hair waving around my face and caught into a loose chignon on top of my head. The prettily coloured clothes I now wore helped as well and my grey eyes took colour from the things I wore. I put my arms round the woman and hugged her.

'I do love you, Mrs Larkin.'

She pushed me away but she was pleased nonetheless.

'Go on now, we'll never get these strawberries done and there's a special evening this evening with high stakes.' And she winked. I felt very conspiratorial, then a thought struck me.

'Mrs Larkin,' I said, 'when I first came here, you remember my stepfather came to take me back?'

She nodded, her lips pursed, so I went on,

'I overheard you and Mr Larkin talking after he'd gone. Mr Larkin was saying that my stepfather had threatened him. Something to do with respectability. Was it the gaming room he was talking about?'

Mrs Larkin nodded again.

'You see, my dear, a small hotel like this doesn't bring in very much if you're only the manager and the gaming room brings in that little extra that makes all the difference.'

'And the gaming room is against the law?'

She stopped what she was doing and turned to me, unusually serious.

'Well, it is and it isn't,' she said. 'You see, if it was just a few guests having a quiet game of cards or some such then that would be all right but we very often have gentlemen who aren't guests in the hotel and some of them like to play for high stakes so I can't say it's strictly legal.'

'And my stepfather was threatening to tell the owners of the hotel?' I said.

Mrs Larkin laughed.

'Oh, the owners know all right, my dear. They take half the profits from it. No, it's the police he was going to tell and then the owners would say they knew nothing about it and Larkin and I would be out of a job.'

'But that's unfair!' I cried.

She shrugged,

'Life's unfair, my dear. It was part of the job when Larkin took over the hotel. He knew it was take it or leave it.'

'And if the authorities get to know it'll be you who suffer?'

She patted my hand. 'Now don't you go worrying yourself. Nobody's going to get to know about it. It's very quiet and very select. Why, even you didn't know it was going on all these months and you've been living here.'

I saw that she was right. The entrance to the little room at the back was separate from the main hotel entrance and it must indeed be run very quietly, but I still felt very humble when I realised what a risk they were taking keeping me here after the threats made by Mr Petheridge.

It was some weeks later that Mr Larkin took ill. It was nothing, he said, but he looked quite grey and Mrs Larkin packed him off to bed. She looked worried.

'It's an important evening in the gaming room,' she said softly to me as we came downstairs, 'a private function and we'd been hoping to build these kind of evenings into a regular thing. That's why Larkin's so worried.'

Mr Larkin always handled the money on these occasions, sitting behind a desk on a dais at one end of the room and looking very important and superior in his stiff shirt and buttonhole as he exchanged money for chips and paid out the winnings.

'I'll do it, Mrs Larkin,' I said. 'You know I'm good with figures.'

She looked shocked.

'You'll do no such thing, a young lady of good breeding. It's no place for you.'

I wore her down eventually for there was no one else to take Mr Larkin's place and that evening I came downstairs ready to take my place behind the great desk. I was wearing my most sophisticated gown. It was of grey watered silk and had a high frilled collar and sleeves to the wrist. Colours flashed from it as the silk caught the light and were reflected in my eyes.

'Well now, don't you look a treat,' said Mrs Larkin.

'And perfectly respectable too, Mrs Larkin, so you need have no fears.'

The gaming room was a blaze of light as I entered, and if Ben, the doorman, thought it odd that I should preside for the evening he made no comment but bowed me to my place as if I were royalty. My appearance caused a stir throughout the room and I saw several appreciative looks cast in my direction. My legs felt unsteady as I stood up to explain the absence of Mr Larkin but the room was not large and my voice carried easily through it. As I spoke I was amused to notice the speculative gleam die out of eyes here and there and was glad of my 'lady's' voice and manner for I knew that to be here, a lone woman, presiding over a company of men engaged in games of chance would cause eyebrows to be raised even in the most advanced of drawing rooms.

I sat down and the evening's proceedings began. I was nervous but running under the nervousness was a thin thread of excitement that came to me from the floor of the room — the thrill of chance. I shivered as it seemed to touch me and I knew my cheeks were bright with excitement. As I looked across the room I noticed a man watching me. He was tall and broad, his fair hair striking against the dark cloth of his evening clothes. He bowed and smiled and his face was so open, so laughing, that I was reminded swiftly of my father and a tiny flame of joy leapt up in me. I smiled back and bowed in turn then my attention was required for my duties.

The evening was well advanced when it happened. There was a scuffle at the door and I looked up. It was my stepfather. I watched motionless as he advanced towards me until his face filled the whole of my vision. I felt sick. I tried to stand but my legs would not support me. He was mouthing at me, shouting obscenities. I put my hands to my ears to stop myself hearing but I could not help it. All around people were standing or sitting stock-still, their faces turned towards us.

'Like father, like daughter,' he was shouting, 'and worse more likely in a place like this. She's gone now. My sister. My keeper,' his face was thrust into mine as he said with great deliberation, 'she cannot keep me away from you any more. I'll not let you rest, Felicia, my lovely Felicia. We shall see how you compare with your mother.' And one of those horrible hands came up and touched my hair. I remember thinking — he is mad, quite mad. Then suddenly there was another figure there. I saw the fair head, heard the muttered oath as he swung my stepfather round by his coat collar and cast him to the floor like so much debris. Then I fled.

I had no idea where I was going. I only know that I ran from the room and into the street and did not stop until I could no longer go on. I leaned against what I thought was a wall and stumbled, grasping it for support, but it was not a wall, it was the parapet of a bridge. Below me the waters of the Thames slid past in a pale sheet. It looked so calm, so peaceful. I suddenly felt very tired. The parapet was quite low and I put my hands flat on top of it. I thought of my stepfather and the fact that his sister was, presumably, dead since she was no longer there to keep him from me. I thought of the Larkins and the trouble he would make for them now. I pushed myself out. I felt the air cool on my cheeks, saw the water shining, inviting. Then my arm was gripped in a hand like steel and I was pulled away, back onto solid ground.

'You little fool,' said a voice and I looked up into the face of the fair man. I felt faint. I remember saying,

'It looked so calm, so quiet,' and then I must indeed have fainted.

When I opened my eyes it was to feel a man's arms around me and I began to tremble violently.

'Hush now,' said a voice very gently and I looked up into the face of the stranger. I tried to speak but no words would come so he picked me up as if I weighed no more than a feather and carried me back to the hotel.

I don't remember exactly how many days I kept to my bed, only that each day the stranger came to visit, bringing small gifts of flowers or sweets when he came. At first I was silent, listening as he spoke to me, but gradually I began to talk and somehow with him it was not difficult to speak of the fear I had of my stepfather and the life I had led. I found that I was able to tell him all the things I had been unable to tell the Larkins and for the first time in many years I felt clean, purged of all those dreadful memories. His eyes were full of sympathy but laughter was never far from the surface and soon he had me laughing too. His name was Charles Allingham, and he was in London on behalf of his brother's business affairs.

I heard snatches of conversation between him and the Larkins outside my door.

'She is much distressed by what has happened.' This was Charles.

'Indeed sir and it's no wonder. The man is a fiend and I understand his sister is no longer alive or he would be kept in check,' replied Mrs Larkin.

And again,

'He hates her, sir. It's his pleasure to make people afraid of him and she has always stood out against him in her way. I remember when he first came to the house after her mother died. Her poor mother, what could she do with a child and nothing to live on?'

And once,

'Would she be agreeable, do you think?'

'Well, sir, it certainly seems a solution and the family is well known. You go ahead and write to your brother.'

All this I heard but took little notice of. I had got up and was sitting in the little parlour one morning when he arrived. I was still pale but he could bring the colour to my cheeks with his fun and nonsense. I rose to greet him.

'You spend far too much of your time coming to visit me.'

He took my hand in both of his and looked into my face. Laughter danced behind his eyes.

'This is true, Felicia, but then London is so dull at this time of year. It's either you or Kew Gardens, and flowers make me sneeze.'

I laughed up at him. 'You must have completed your business by now.'

He was suddenly serious. 'Yes, and that's why I've come.'

He drew me to a chair and made me sit. 'Felicia, I am not happy leaving you in London.'

I shivered in spite of the warmth of the room. Fear of meeting my stepfather had made me keep to the hotel and I had not realised how much I depended on Charles's visits, not only for the pleasure of his company but from the sense of safety that I felt knowing that he was in London. The thought of his leaving filled me with dread. But he was still speaking.

'I have spoken to the Larkins and they have agreed that you should no longer remain here.'

I was shocked. 'But where would I go?'

He smiled. 'That is what I wanted to talk to you about.' He drew his chair closer. 'I have told you of my home at Dryford?'

I nodded. He had described what sounded a lovely old house in the Scottish Borders, where he lived with his brother and nephew. Keep Dryford, it was called and I had teased him about being a Border Reiver. I did so again and he smiled.

'Not me,' he said, 'I'm the English brother. Very respectable.'

He looked down at his hands then up again, before I could ask him what he meant.

'My brother's wife has been ill. She has been away from home for some time but is expected back quite soon. The child is still young, only eight, and needs someone to look after him. Also he needs some schooling. His nurse, who was our nurse too, will be kept busy looking after my brother's wife once she comes home so you see, there is a place for you there if you wish it.'

My hand still rested in his and I looked up at him.

'Leave the Larkins?' I said.

'For a new life,' he answered. His gaze was very steady. I was confused.

'I shall need time to think about it,' I said.

'Of course, but not too much time, Felicia. If you do decide to come it would be better if you travelled with me.'

'When do you leave?' I asked.

He looked a little rueful. 'Tomorrow,' he said, 'or at the latest the day after. I really should have been home some days ago.'

I was immediately contrite. 'And you stayed just to come and see me?'

He laughed. 'Oh, London has many pleasures,' he said. 'Don't go thinking you're its only attraction.'

I laughed, feeling easier, then I thought of the risk to the Larkins' security if I stayed with them. My stepfather would not let them rest as long as I was here. All at once my mind was made up.

'I'll come,' I said.

The Larkins, though sorry to see me go, were pleased at the way things had turned out.

'It's more fitting for a young lady than what you're doing here, Miss Felicia,' said Mrs Larkin.

'You'll be all right there,' said Mr Larkin. 'I have a letter from Mr Allingham's brother, and he seems a proper gentleman.'

'Oh, Mr Larkin,' I said, 'did you ask for a testimonial?'

'Indeed I did, my dear, as is only right and proper.'

He showed me the letter and it was indeed extremely proper. It referred to me throughout as 'the young person' and made it quite clear that as he had not met me the position would be reviewed after a month to the 'satisfaction of both parties'.

'Good gracious,' I said, 'he sounds quite fierce.'

'He's quite right, my dear,' said Mrs Larkin, 'he has a child's welfare to consider and that's no light matter.'

I felt suitably chastened, then my attention was caught by the sprawling signature. I could not make it out but one thing was certain. It was not Allingham. I remembered Charles's reference to his being the 'English brother' and I determined to ask him about it.

I got the opportunity next day on the long train journey north.

'Why is your brother's name different to yours?' Charles smiled.

'He's actually my half-brother. Same mother, different fathers. He's a few years older than me.'

'Is that why you call yourself the English brother?'

'Yes, my mother was a Scot but my father was English. Lachlan on the other hand is pure Scot.'

'Lachlan,' I repeated. 'That's a strange name.'

'Och aye, lassie, it's no' sae strange whaur you're gaun,' he said in a travesty of a Scots accent and I laughed.

'Tell me about him,' I said, 'this Lachlan,' and the word sounded strange on my lips, 'and about Keep Dryford. That doesn't sound so terribly Scottish.'

Charles leaned back and began to speak.

'It is in Scotland but only just. The land round about was fought over for centuries by those Border Reivers you seem to find so romantic, though I don't think it could have been as romantic as you think. Dryford was razed to the ground several times in the course of history and had to be rebuilt. The present house is only about two hundred years old. It's built inside a loop of the River Tweed, for defence I suppose, hence the name. Before the  estate bridges were built there was only one access to it. The Grants have lived there for generations. It came to Lachlan through my mother's family. As heir he took the family name for his own.'

'So his father's name was different again?'

Charles smiled.

'Confusing, isn't it? But mother was the last of the Grants and she held the estate in trust for the elder son.'

'And didn't your father mind, his son not taking his name?'

'Not my father, Lachlan's,' Charles corrected me. 'My father was an Allingham from Sussex. I didn't know Lachlan's father, of course; he died when Lachlan was very young so I don't know if he minded or not, but Keep Dryford could never belong to anyone other than a Grant.'

'So you . . . '

'Will never be Master of Keep Dryford,' he finished for me. 'No the next Master will be Alexander, Lachlan's son. I am merely the poor half-brother.'

I was on the point of laughing at his dramatic view of himself when I noticed the tightness about his mouth.

'Does it hurt?' I asked gently.

He smiled and the tightness was gone.

'The plight of the younger brother is rather too common to be of much interest, Felicia. Let's just say it irritates me sometimes.'

'What was he like, your father?' I said.

'As unlike Lachlan's I gather as it was possible to be and, I suspect, a great deal more fun.'

'And your mother, she was happy with both?'

He considered this.

'I think my mother was rather like one of those strange creatures you see at the Zoological Gardens. A chameleon, it's called. It changes the colour of its skin depending on its background. I've no reason to believe she was not happy with both.'

The tightness about his mouth was returning so I did not pursue the point.

'Your brother, what's he like?'

33

He laughed. 'Like our fathers, he is as unlike me as it is possible to be. Very worthy.'

I laughed too. 'Then I shall not like him at all.'

He looked serious then, and took my hand.

'Oh, but you must, Felicia, for if you did not then you might go away, and I should be heartbroken.'

I felt my heart give a little leap then I noticed the twinkle at the back of his eyes and scolded him.

'Can you never be serious?'

'Never,' he said.

I asked him about his brother's wife but he was strangely evasive.

'It's an odd situation,' he said, 'and not a very happy one. She was much upset by the death of her sister last year and has been only recently back to their family home in Italy where the accident happened. I'm not quite sure when she is expected at Dryford.'

'She is Italian then?' I said in surprise.

He nodded. 'Yes, we were all somewhat surprised at Lachlan's choice.' He looked out of the window at the passing countryside and I barely heard his words as he said, 'I wonder if he is regretting it now,' then he turned to me smiling and said,

'Now who else can I tell you about? Oh, yes, Alexander, the child. He's eight now and an exact replica of his father. Very serious.' He pulled a face at me and I laughed.

'Then he should not be troublesome.'

'I shouldn't count on that, Felicia, he's rather an odd child in some ways but you must judge for yourself.' He went on, 'And then of course there's Araminta.'

'Araminta?' I repeated.

Charles was looking out of the window again at the rolling hills.

'A sort of cousin of Lachlan's. She's not yet eighteen and he's her guardian. She's an orphan as well as an heiress so you see he does have a highly-developed sense of duty,' and he gave a little laugh. 'You will find that my dear half-brother is something of a paragon, Felicia.'

'He sounds extremely dull,' I said.

He gave me a quick look and smiled.

'Oh, Felicia, I shall so enjoy you being at Dryford.'

I felt my cheeks flush with pleasure at his words and encouraged him to speak further of what I should find there, and I heard of the old nurse Dorcas who had been with the family since Lachlan was a baby; of a brother and sister called Sutherland who were living not far from Keep Dryford; of old Redpath — man of all work and the source of much folklore. When he had finished detailing the household I said,

'Quite a large house then?'

'I'm sure you'll find us very provincial after London,' he teased.

I looked at him closely.

'Do you like living at Dryford, Charles?' I asked.

For a moment I thought he would not answer, then he said, 'My dear, I have no choice.' And there was a bitter twist to his mouth.

He seemed disinclined for conversation after that so I turned my attention to the scenery flying past outside. The neat fields of the South had long since given way to rolling hills and then to what seemed to me mountains. I had never seen such country. Even the air seemed sharper, clearer somehow and with an edge to it though we were in high summer. After the stuffiness of London I found it invigorating. And so I sat at the window and wondered what was in front of me and thought of all that had gone before and the events that had led me to Keep Dryford.

# 2

There was a carriage at the station to meet us. It was driven by an old man with a weatherbeaten face and startlingly blue eyes.

'Good-day, Mr Charles,' he said, 'and I hope ye've had a good journey.'

Then to me, 'Good-day, Miss, and welcome to Dryford.'

His voice had a strong Scottish accent that sounded strange in my ears but his eyes were kindly and I felt reassured by his welcome.

It was not a long drive and the sun was low in the sky as we drove in through the gates of Keep Dryford. There was a bank of trees to the right which obscured the house but when we had rounded them I caught my breath. There is stood as it had done for at least two centuries, its lawns smooth and green, sloping down to the broad expanse of shining water which was the River Tweed. The house itself stood, as Charles had said, in a wide loop of the river, almost an island, its only approach by land being the way we had come. I could see several low stone bridges spanning the water at various points.

My eye took in its towers and battlements, its turrets and windows cut deeply into the stone. Only the height and width of those windows reminded me that it was not as old as it first appeared.

'You did not tell me it was a castle,' I said accusingly.

'Only a small one,' said Charles modestly, 'but fit for a small princess.'

His eyes were bright with laughter.

I was nervous as Charles handed me down from the carriage. I looked at the imposing archway which surmounted a flight of worn stone steps and drew a deep breath as I started up them. The great oak door was thrown open as I was halfway up and a figure stood for a moment in the doorway before it flung itself in a whirl of bright beauty down the steps and into Charles's arms.

'Oh, Charles, it's so good to have you home again. Things are so dull here when you're away.'

I stood transfixed for a moment taking in the spun gold hair cascading from its restraining pins, the swirl of the pretty pink muslin gown and the sea-blue eyes that looked up at him accusingly over a petulant mouth. Charles held her away from him, laughing.

'And this, Felicia, is my dear cousin Araminta.'

I made to stretch out my hand in greeting. I had never felt so dowdy as I did then in my brown merino travelling dress, my hair pushed firmly back under my bonnet. A deep, slightly cold voice interrupted,

'Araminta, you really should not throw yourself at Charles that way. You will give our new governess a totally unsuitable impression of our manners here.'

I felt my cheeks flush at the word. I suppose I had known from the beginning that I was to be governess to the child but Charles had never referred to it as such. It had been as if I were coming as his friend rather than as his brother's employee. I felt myself withdraw slightly as I turned to the speaker.

'I assure you, sir, I do not make up my mind hastily about such matters.'

He was tall and broad and his hair was as dark as his brother's was fair. From my position halfway down the steps he had an air of command that was not lightened by his expression. He came down the steps towards me.

'Miss Grainger, I am pleased to make your acquaintance and delighted that you have such a sensible approach to life.'

He flicked a glance at the other two. 'Araminta, perhaps you will be so good as to show Miss Grainger to her rooms.'

'Oh, Lachlan,' she said, her blue eyes clouding, 'can't Dorcas do that? Charles has only just arrived and I did so want to ask him about London.'

His voice was cool but firm.

'I too want to ask him about London,' he said, 'and I rather think my questions will be more pertinent than yours. Now run along.' He turned to Charles. 'The library, I think.'

Charles shot me a look as he passed to follow his brother inside. It was so comical I giggled. Araminta looked at me critically.

'Well, I suppose you'll have to do. You tell me about London.'

I looked at her in surprise but she seemed totally unaware of her rudeness and her eyes began to sparkle as she plied me with questions about the latest fashions, the theatres, the shops. I'm afraid I could tell her very little about these things and she stamped her foot in vexation.

'Oh, Lachlan is such a bore.' Then, 'Never mind, I shall have Charles all to myself soon and he always has lots to tell me. He goes to the most exciting places.'

By this time we had arrived on the second floor and she threw open a door on our right.

'This is yours,' she said waving an arm around. 'You'll be quite comfortable while you're here, though I don't suppose that'll be for long.'

I looked at her in amazement. She really was an outspoken person.

'What makes you say that?' I said, curious.

She was in the act of closing the door on her way out.

'They never do,' she said. 'It depends what type they are. Either they fall in love with Charles or they fall in love with Lachlan and then, of course, they have to go.'

She looked at me closely, her beautiful blue eyes narrowing like a kitten's.

'I wonder which type you are,' she said. Then she turned on her heel and was gone. As she went the words came floating back through the half-open door.

'And, besides, Alexander isn't exactly a nursemaid's dream. He's an odd little thing.'

I sat down on a chair, torn between irritation and amusement. First a governess and now a nursemaid. And what on earth did 'odd' mean? Charles too had referred to the child as odd. I took off my bonnet and looked round. I was in a spacious sitting room, its windows looking over the lawns to the river, and in the distance the hills rose blue and misty to the sky. There was a bedroom adjoining the sitting room and hot water and towels had been laid out by some thoughtful person.

I felt better after I had washed and changed out of my heavy travelling dress and into a lighter one. I chose a pale mauve muslin with a demure white collar in recognition of my status. I brushed my hair and secured it firmly, hoping that I looked every inch the governess, then I went in search of my employer.

If I had thought I would have difficulty finding the library then I was I mistaken. There was no one in the hall and through the slightly-open door the words came clearly.

'She'll make a wonderful governess.' This was Charles, defensive. Then came his brother's voice, low but penetrating.

'And did it not occur to you that I should have the privilege of choosing for myself my son's governess?'

'You could have refused.'

'My dear Charles, I was presented with a *fait accompli*, and how you persuaded her guardians to let her come with you, a stranger . . . '

'She has no guardians. She is alone in the world.'

There was a small silence. Then,

'I see,' he said, and at the tone I felt my face flame.

Charles was speaking again. 'You'll see for yourself at dinner. She's a wonderful girl.'

'Governesses do not usually dine with the family, Charles.'

'This governess is different, Lachlan. She's from a good family, she's not used to being treated like a servant.'

I thought of my years in my stepfather's house and my heart went out in gratitude to Charles for his defence, but he was speaking still.

'You cannot expect her to dine in her room with a tray.' His voice was contemptuous.

'I shall not comment on her 'difference' to other women, Charles, or on the fact that being a 'wonderful girl' is perhaps not the best recommendation for a governess. I think you know my attitude towards your susceptibilities, but surely if she is so unused to being treated as a servant she ought not to have become a governess.'

Charles started to speak again but Lachlan seemed to have grown tired of the conversation.

'Oh, have it your own way,' he said curtly. 'There are other more important things to discuss.'

I fled back the way I had come, my cheeks still burning and the thought in my head — what did he mean by a *fait accompli?* He had written expressing his agreement with the arrangement, then a suspicion flashed across my mind. I remembered Charles's words.

'Don't worry about a thing. I'll write to him.' And when the letter had come, 'Didn't I tell you it would be fine?'

Oh no, I thought, he can't have. But by then I had reached my own room and there was a sound of movement.

The child was standing by the window, his hand fingering the heavy curtain, and as he turned I felt the breath catch at the emptiness of the blue-grey eyes. His hair was as dark as his father's but his face was pale and set and it was void of all expression.

'You must be Alexander?' I said.

'You are the new governess,' he said and his voice, too, was curiously flat.

I smiled but there was no answering smile in his eyes and his face remained grave. I had the feeling that I must be very careful to make no sudden movement. It was as if I had come across some frightened animal in a forest though no fear showed itself in those eyes, only a great emptiness. I held out my hand but he made no move to put his out though he was standing facing me. It was only then that I realised with a shock that the child was blind.

'How do you do,' he was saying gravely.

'Would you care to sit down?' I said and wondered at myself. I was treating an eight-year-old child like an adult and all the time trying to come to terms with the fact of his blindness.

He shook his head. 'No thank you,' he said, 'I merely wished to meet you.'

'But perhaps we could have a talk,' I said. 'We could get to know each other.'

His eyes seemed to be upon me and I shivered.

'There is no point,' he said. 'You will not be here for long.'

Before I could answer the door was opened and a shadow fell across us. 'It's time for your supper, Master Alexander,' said a voice.

'Yes, Dorcas,' the child said and walked obediently and unerringly towards the door. He turned on the threshold and spoke to me.

'The schoolroom is on the floor above,' he said, 'I shall be there at ten o'clock tomorrow morning if that will be convenient.'

He closed the door behind him softly and I turned to the woman beside me. It must have shown in my face.

'No one told you,' she said.

'No,' I whispered. 'I'm sorry but it has come as something of a shock.'

'Aye,' she said, nodding her head. 'It would do. They should have told you. Still you're here now so you'll just have to get used to it.'

She was a severe looking woman with hair that had been dark going grey now but her eyes were bright as she looked at me. 'You think him strange?' she said.

I hardly knew how to answer.

'He seems remarkably composed for such a young child,' I said, 'and . . . and very able to get around . . . ' my voice trailed off.

She nodded again.

'You think he's odd, I can see. Well judge not is what I say lest you yourself be judged.' She looked at me almost fiercely. 'And you need have no fear for him going about the place. He knows the house and grounds better than the rest of us put together. It's not natural the way that laddie can get around, and him so afflicted. Ach well, you'll find that out for yourself so I'll say goodnight and I hope you'll be comfortable while you're here.' And then she, too, was gone.

I sat down at once and looked out of the window. The river gleamed in the evening light and the scene was one of peace and beauty. I thought of my reception in this odd household and remarked under my breath that it hardly seemed worth while unpacking. I was clearly not expected to stay. When Araminta burst into the room and flung herself into the chair opposite I could have hugged her. She seemed almost normal now.

'Well,' she said, 'there was a storm about it but you're to dine as family so we'd better see what you've got that's fit to wear.'

I could not help it, I burst out laughing at her audacity. I laughed till the tears spilled down my cheeks. Perhaps it was reaction.

'Good gracious,' she said regarding me suspiciously, 'I do believe you're as odd as the rest of us. Well, come on, what have you got? You certainly can't come down in that. You look like a parlourmaid.'

She threw open my trunk and began to rummage in it, pulling out clothes and casting them about the room.

'The Sutherlands are coming tonight so you really should wear something decent. They're our nearest neighbours. There's Douglas who's very serious and quiet and Alison who looks serious and quiet but isn't.' She turned mischievous eyes on me. 'She's in love with Lachlan.'

I was shocked. Although I knew from Charles that she was only two years younger than me she seemed much more irresponsible.

'Araminta,' I said.

She looked at me critically, her head on one side and said,

'Yes, I suppose you'd better call me Araminta. It would look pretty silly if you were to call me Miss Araminta this and Miss Araminta that across the dinner table.'

My expression must have shown my disapproval for she threw down a pile of underthings and put her hands on her hips. She looked exceedingly pretty.

'Oh, for goodness' sake, don't look so pious. After all it isn't as if you're even a real governess. We all know that was just a trick so that Charles could get you here.'

I made to protest but she was still rattling on.

'And besides, it's true. She's been in love with him for years. At one time it was thought they'd marry. It would have been a good match with the estates adjoining each other but then Lachlan went abroad for a while and lo and behold he brought back a wife. It was terribly romantic'

She collapsed on a pile of clothes, and I groaned inwardly as I thought how crushed they would be.

'It was in Venice,' she said, her eyes dreamy. 'Can you imagine it? So romantic. Gondolas and serenades and the waters of the lagoon glinting in the moonlight.'

I tried to imagine Lachlan Grant serenading his lady love from a gondola and failed completely. She looked at me sharply.

'He wasn't always like this, you know. When I was fourteen I was quite in love with him myself. But that was before the tragedy.'

'Tragedy?' I said.

She nodded.

'It happened last year. Vida's sister was killed while she was on a visit to her family home in Italy. She used to be such a sweet person but she's different now. Everything's different now.' Araminta jumped up. 'This will do,' she said, holding up my grey silk, 'I'd better change or we'll be late. Don't take for ever. I'll come and fetch you on my way down.'

She left my mind in as great a muddle as she left my room and by the time I had tidied up I did not have much time to dress. I loosened my hair and brushed it, pinning it more loosely on top of my head so that the waves framed and softened my face. I picked up the pale grey silk that I had not worn since the evening of my encounter with Charles. I shivered slightly as I put it on and told myself not to be foolish, then the thought of seeing Charles again brought the colour to my cheeks until I remembered the conversation I had overheard in the library. I would have to speak to him.

I must confess that I looked with interest at the dinner guests that night. Douglas Sutherland was a man in his early thirties, quiet with a kind face and brown eyes and hair. He greeted me with a deference that contrasted oddly with both the affectionate familiarity of Charles and the cool politeness of his brother. Alison Sutherland was a feminine version of her brother with smooth brown hair and gentle eyes. At first she seemed rather colourless, but as dinner progressed I noticed an undertone of red in that smooth brown hair that gave it a curious vibrancy and her eyes though brown were not the soft brown of her brother's. They were like dark pools, looking almost black at times. She was not conventionally pretty but there was something about her that belied that first impression of ordinariness and I thought of Araminta's words — she looks serious and quiet but isn't. Her gown too, at first sight, looked almost dull until she moved in it and whether it was the cut of the gown or her own natural grace I could not tell., but I wondered how I could even for a moment have thought the rather dark blue watered silk dull. It occurred to me that she was a very sophisticated woman. She must have been six or seven years younger than her brother and whereas Araminta made me feel quite elderly, she made me feel like a child.

The conversation flowed easily after an initial gaffe by Araminta.

'Here we are, then,' she said as we sat down, 'Lachlan, Alison, Charles, Felicia, Douglas and me. You balance up the numbers nicely, Felicia, though what we'll do when Vida comes home I don't know.'

The reactions of the rest were interesting. Lachlan Grant looked irritated, Charles amused, Douglas gently reproachful and Alison concerned. She turned to me.

'You will get used to Araminta's outspokenness in time, Miss Grainger.'

Her manner was almost proprietorial as she smiled at Lachlan, and I saw him relax slightly. Douglas leaned towards me and said, 'She is our 'enfant terrible'.'

Araminta flashed him a look. 'Not such a child, Douglas; after all I'm nearly eighteen.'

He looked slightly discomfitted as her smile became mischievous and Charles interrupted.

'Perhaps when you're eighteen you'll start behaving like a young lady.'

She looked at him from beneath impossibly long lashes. 'And who's to teach me?'

He laughed. 'Perhaps Felicia will.' And he raised his glass to me.

I smiled back but his brother interrupted.

'I am sure Miss Grainger will be fully occupied with Alexander,' he said to Charles.

And to me, 'Perhaps after dinner you would come to the library, Miss Grainger. I should like to discuss my son's education with you.'

I inclined my head, conscious of the fact that for him at least I was not a guest at the table.

Over dinner I learned something of the history of the area which had in past centuries been turbulent and bloody.

'I've never understood why the Grants were not knighted at least,' said Charles. 'After all a castle deserves something more than a plain Mister.'

'But we Grants are Masters of Dryford,' said Lachlan drily, 'a curiously Scottish invention and besides the Grants were always too busy keeping the ravening hordes of Englishmen from our door to have time to dally at Court seeking favours.'

Charles turned to me.

'Didn't I tell you, Felicia? Pure Scot. It must make Dryford's past Masters turn in their graves to see an Englishman living at the Keep.'

'Come now, Charles,' said his brother, 'you are too sensitive and, besides, you have our mother's Scottish blood in your veins.'

Their manner was light enough but there was an undercurrent of strain and Alison turned the conversation neatly.

'You will not have had time yet to seel the Keep, Miss Grainger. It is the only part of the original buildings still standing.'

'Indeed at one time it was the only building,' said Lachlan. 'I don't know if you are familiar with these old Border Keeps, Miss Grainger?'

I shook my head. 'I'm ashamed to confess that I know nothing of them at all, Mr Grant,' I said.

'Then we must set that to rights at once,' he said, and went on to speak of the subject with such authority and knowledge that I found myself fascinated by it.

'Strictly speaking it is not a keep at all, Miss Grainger,' he began.

'Oh Lachlan, don't be pedantic,' said Charles. 'Felicia isn't interested in the history of architecture. She wants to hear stories of Border raids and maidens being abducted by wild Scotsmen, don't you, Felicia?' And he laid his hand on mine.

'Indeed I am interested in history,' I protested, 'and in architecture and I'll warrant most of the stories you'd tell me would be grossly exaggerated.'

Araminta squeaked with delight and Charles subsided, his dignity momentarily offended as I turned eagerly to the man they called the Master of Dryford,

'The Tower of London is a keep, isn't it, one of the earliest?'

He looked at me with approval and no little surprise.

'Yes indeed,' he said, 'but that was built long before our modest Dryford.'

'And what is Dryford if not a keep?' I said, leaning forward.

'It's what is known in Scotland as a Tower House,' he continued. 'Some say they were modelled on the Norman keeps that were introduced to England in the Middle Ages, some that they are related to the much earlier brochs or circular stone towers of Scotland. I think ours is rather closer to the latter.'

The Scottish burr was more pronounced now and I found it oddly attractive.

'They were built, as Charles so romantically puts it, at the time of the Border raids in the sixteenth century as both defence against attack and living quarters. If you imagine a house built one room on top of the other you will have some idea of the architecture of the Tower House.'

'And did they pour boiling oil down on the enemy as Charles says?' asked Araminta, her eyes shining. 'And bring the pigs and cows into the Lord's Hall when the reivers reived or whatever it is reivers do?'

Her guardian looked at her in mild exasperation.

'My dear Araminta . . . '

'Oh don't call me your dear Araminta like that. You make me feel about a hundred years old.'

'Araminta,' he began again patiently, 'the main purpose of the Tower House was, as its name suggests, as a house for living in, not a fortification. It strength lay in the fact that, occupying so little ground and being built several stories high with enormously thick walls, it was almost impregnable. And as for bringing the animals into the Laird's Hall, I doubt if the Laird would have been very pleased. The animals would be brought into the enclosure in which the tower stood, or if necessary into the cellar apartment.'

Araminta looked disappointed. 'I think I prefer Charles's version,' she said. 'Was there nothing romantic about them?'

Lachlan Grant laughed.

'They were reasonably comfortable, defensible and cheap to build — a combination irresistible to any self-respecting Scot.'

'Oh Lachlan, you are so dreary at times. There must be some story attached to the Keep, it's so ancient.'

He appeared to consider this, then said slowly,

55

'There was one but I'm afraid it would frighten you too much.'

'Oh, tell me, tell me, please!' she wheedled. 'I promise I won't be frightened.'

'It was many years ago,' he began, 'at the time of the Border raids when the Tower was first being built. They say the first Master had a beautiful young wife with whom he was madly in love. He was a very proud man and very jealous and he kept her in his tower, only letting her out as the sun went down to gather the sweet herbs she used for her remedies. She was a wonderful herbalist and some say she had made a love potion to ensnare him, so wildly was he in love with her. It was whilst she was gathering her herbs one evening that she was seen by a young nobleman from the other side of the border. He had been out hunting and had followed his prey farther than was wise. When he saw her he was overcome by her beauty and stretching out his arm he lifted her onto the saddle of his horse and bore her away to England.'

Araminta was hardly breathing, her eyes wide with wonder.

'What did her husband do?' she asked.

'He got her back, of course,' said Lachlan Grant. 'After all he was Master of Dryford. He and his men rode across the border and stormed the castle and brought her back to

Dryford.' His voice dropped. 'But it was too late. The Tower was just being completed. It's said that she's there still, walled up in the topmost room.'

Tears stood in Araminta's blue eyes and she said, 'But who was she and why was it too late?'

There was silence in the room and his voice was low.

'At first they did not know what had happened to her, then a shepherd boy came to the Master of Dryford and told him of the young nobleman and the beautiful woman he had seen riding together across the border, but by that time she had been in England too long. Her name was Araminta and she talked too much.'

Araminta stared at him open-mouthed for a moment and then,

'Oh you beast, Lachlan,' she cried, 'you unutterable beast.'

The whole table dissolved into laughter and Alison chided him for baiting Araminta.

'She deserved it,' said Lachlan Grant good-humouredly. 'Romance she wanted and romance she got.'

We took coffee in the drawing room after dinner and I relaxed a little and looked around me. I had found the dining room rather impressive and slightly awe inspiring with its massive oak table and the silver epergne that dominated it, reflecting light from chandeliers. The drawing room, the 'small drawing room' as I later learned to call it, was built and furnished for comfort rather than ceremony, and I leaned back in my deep-buttoned armchair as Charles lit a cigar and propped himself up against the mantelpiece, one foot on the brass fender.

'What shall it be then, charades?'

'Oh Charles, how babyish,' said Araminta. 'I have a much better idea.' And she rushed from the room in a flurry of cream silk flounces.

Alison laughed. 'When will she ever grow up?' she said, looking at Charles.

'Probably never,' replied Charles with a tolerant smile.

'What she needs is a husband,' said his brother from the depths of his armchair.

'Surely not,' broke in Douglas. 'She's too young yet.'

'Nonsense,' said Lachlan Grant. 'She's flighty. The sooner she settles down the better, as far as I'm concerned. It'll be no joke being Araminta's guardian once she comes out. She's the type that needs to marry young, someone dependable who'll take her in hand.'

Alison protested, 'Now really, Lachlan, can you see Araminta allowing anyone to 'take her in hand' as you put it? And besides, Douglas is right; she's too young yet.'

'Now, now, Alison,' said Charles, 'don't argue with Lachlan. After all he should know what he's talking about. He married young enough,' and he cast a look at his brother.

The lines around Lachlan Grant's mouth tightened and I thought Charles had goaded him but he merely flicked the ash casually from his cigar into the fire as he rose from his chair saying to me,

'I have some work to do, Miss Grainger. I'll let you know when I am ready to discuss my son.'

At that moment Araminta hurtled through the door carrying a large book and various pieces of paper and pens. She stopped, crestfallen, as she saw that her guardian was leaving.

'You're not going are you, Lachlan? I wanted you to join in.'

He looked at the book in her hand.

'Why Araminta, I don't believe I've ever seen you in possession of a book before. What's this? Making up for all those misspent schooldays?'

She tossed her head at him and flounced into the room.

'Beast,' she said without rancour, 'don't join in then. Honestly, you get stuffier by the day. Now,' she said to the rest of us, 'I'm going to write all your names down on one piece of paper and their meanings on another and the game is to guess which name goes with which meaning.'

Her expression was so eager that everyone smiled and agreed and she sat down on the floor in a most unladylike fashion and began to look up names in her book and laboriously copy out the meanings.

It was a pleasant enough game if a little childish, but it gave me the opportunity to observe these people who were, except for Charles, strangers to me. There was much hilarity as Charles refused to take it seriously and insisted that 'Araminta' meant 'manly' and was then quite delighted when told that that was what 'Charles' meant. I remember thinking that Alison's name was appropriate enough.

'Noble,' said Araminta, 'or kind, except that I don't know if it's one or the other or both.'

'Oh, Araminta,' said Alison smiling, and I decided that it was probably both.

I was to find during my time at Dryford that it was a constant cry — 'Oh, Araminta!'

'Felicia means 'happy',' said Douglas from his corner by the fire.

'Why how clever,' said Araminta. 'How did you know that, Douglas?'

Douglas smiled gently, 'The benefits of a classical education,' he said.

Araminta shook her head.

'At school we had to guess and guess before we got any right.'

Charles touched my hand. 'Let's go and see the Keep before it gets too dark,' he said softly.

I nodded. 'I'd like to do that,' I said and we rose to go. He turned at the door.

'By the way, what does 'Lachlan' mean?'

'Warlike,' said Araminta with a grimace.

Charles laughed. 'I might have known.'

And so I had my first sight of Keep Dryford against the setting sun and it never looked more beautiful. Standing there, Charles took my hand and slipped it through his arm.

'Does it measure up to your expectations?'

'It's wonderful,' I said. 'How fortunate you are to live here.'

'Even more fortunate now that you're here,' he said softly. I turned to him and out of the corner of my eye caught the glow of a cigar.

'I hate to interrupt, but when you're ready, Miss Grainger,' said Lachlan Grant, as he turned and walked back towards the house.

He was waiting for me in the library, standing by the window which gave onto the lawns. It was not yet entirely dark and there was no light in the room apart from the soft twilight which seemed to linger so much longer here than in the South. He turned as I entered.

'Please, Miss Grainger, be seated.'

I sat but he did not. He seemed to be having some difficulty over what he wanted to say. He picked up a heavy paperweight from the desk and regarded it thoughtfully.

'I believe you have already met my son.'

I assented.

'What did you think of him?'

I hesitated, somewhat taken aback by his directness. How could I say 'I did not know your son was blind'?

'Our meeting was brief,' I said, 'but I found him extremely polite and seemingly mature for his years.'

He fingered the paperweight.

'Seemingly mature,' he repeated and the emphasis was on the first word. Then he put the paperweight back on the desk with great deliberation and thrust his hands deep in his pockets, turning away from me as he did so.

'You too are very polite. Miss Grainger. The truth is my son is not like normal children and has not been so for over a year now and I do not refer merely to his blindness.'

He turned to me almost accusingly.

'You will have heard of the accident?' His voice had the faint burr of the Scot and was oddly clear. I found myself hesitating again.

'Araminta did say . . . ' I began.

He turned sharply away once again.

'In that case perhaps it would be better if I told you the story. My ward is apt to be inaccurate as well as over-dramatic'

I smiled to myself as I thought of Araminta's extravagance of speech but he was speaking again, his voice matter-of-fact to the point of remoteness.

'Until a year ago my son was as normal children, happy, carefree, mischievous. He was no saint but neither was he the withdrawn and 'seemingly mature' child that you saw today.' His voice dwelt on my words. 'At the time of the accident he was staying at my wife's family home in the North of Italy. She was in the habit of making yearly visits home but this was the first time Alexander had accompanied her. My wife, her sister and Alexander went on a picnic. It was a beautiful day and Alexander and his aunt had tethered their horses. My wife was about to dismount. Alexander had run down to the lakeside as

63

children will. Vida was a very fine rider and her mount was a spirited animal.' He was speaking now as if in a dream, looking out of the window as if it were all happening there in the gathering dusk. 'There was a shot, someone on the lake after geese. The horse bolted, became uncontrollable and Alexander saw his aunt crushed to death beneath the hooves of her sister's horse.'

There was silence in the room. It was almost dark now and I struggled to find words to express my sorrow while in my mind I could see the scene; the bright day, the picnic tea laid out on the grass and the rearing, frightened animal, its hooves flailing above the body of a young woman while the child watched from the lakeside. But Alexander was blind. Lachlan was speaking again quietly in the darkness.

'Alexander was in shock for days. The shooting party heard his screams from across the lake and got there as quickly as they could but it took some time. The hunters spoke no English. They found him alone with the body. The horse had bolted. It was some time before it could be brought under control. Both rider and horse were found some time later wandering lost in the hills. Alexander was taken to my wife's family home. He was in such distress that it was only when the doctor arrived that they found out he was blind. There is no medical reason for it. He suffered no injury, no physical injury that is. The doctors say that his blindness is a direct result of the shock. There is nothing wrong with his eyes. He merely does not want to see. It is not usual but I am assured that such cases have been known. He may recover spontaneously, he may not. In any case there is nothing to be done. So you see, Miss Grainger, why Alexander is not like other children?'

I could not speak. There seemed nothing to say. He had turned towards me again but the room was in darkness now and his face was only a pale blur.

'But surely when his mother returns . . . '

He interrupted me smoothly.

'Alexander has not spoken to his mother except by way of polite conversation since that day.'

I gasped. 'But he cannot blame her?'

'Nevertheless that is how the matter stands. There have been other governesses in the past year, Miss Grainger, but none have stayed longer than a few weeks. The longest I recall was three months.' Lachlan sounded bitter, as well he might, as he continued, 'That is why I have asked you to see me this evening. Had I had the opportunity of interviewing you myself I would of course have explained the circumstances to you. As it is you are quite free to decline the position if you so wish. It is not the best situation for a young person in her first post as governess. My brother is apt to be somewhat hasty in his actions and if you do not feel up to the task no doubt he will wish you to stay on for a few weeks as his guest. You are, I understand, a friend of his?'

It was on the tip of my tongue to explain to him what I believed to be the truth about my appointment as governess but I did not judge it to be the right time. It seemed just at that moment to be supremely unimportant. All I could think of was the poor unhappy child and the horror he had experienced.

'I shall be glad to stay as governess,' I heard myself say, 'and I assure you I shall do everything in my power to make Alexander forget that tragic day.'

I could not see his face, standing as he was with his back to the faint light from the window, but I sensed a new warmth in his voice as he said,

'I believe you will, Miss Grainger, and I hope you succeed. I very much fear that it is a friend that Alexander needs more than a governess.'

I rose to take my leave but his voice stayed me.

'One thing you should know, Miss Grainger. Alexander has never spoken of the events of that day. The doctors think that it is quite possible he remembers nothing of it, that he has closed his mind to what happened that day just as he has closed his eyes to the world around him.'

'I understand,' I said, 'and I repeat that I will do my best for Alexander.'

He nodded his dismissal and I left him in the darkness, looking out on the moonlit garden.

It was a long time before I could sleep that night, my emotions were aroused to such a pitch. One moment I was furious with Charles for not telling me the truth about my charge, the next I was overcome with pity for the child; and under it all lay the feeling that I had come to a house of secrets. Charles who in his charming insouciance had already deceived me on two counts; Araminta who could be so amusing and yet so uncaring; Lachlan Grant who had seemed so cold and remote even when speaking of his little son. The faces whirled across my mind like dancers in a tableau but it was not of any of these that I dreamed when eventually I fell asleep. Instead the faces I saw were those of Dorcas, her bright eyes burning into mine, and a shadowy figure that I knew was Vida though the face was Alison Sutherland's.

# 3

I found Alexander in the schoolroom next morning at ten o'clock as he had promised I should. I was nervous of my ability to teach a blind child and I think he sensed this for, going towards a cupboard, he began to pull out some large heavy looking books. I moved to help him but he said clearly enough,

'Please do not trouble, I can manage. You will find that I manage very well in the circumstances.'

He put the books on the table, saying as he did so,

'These are my school books. They are in Braille. Do you know about Braille?'

I found myself answering him as I would have done an adult. He really did have a very mature manner.

'I have heard of it of course, but I have never seen a Braille book.'

He continued to speak as he lugged the books one by one out of the cupboard and piled them on the table. I was surprised at the confidence of his movements.

'It was invented by a blind Frenchman called Louis Braille,' he said, 'about fifty years ago. The Braille alphabet consists of one to five raised dots embossed in the paper and arranged differently for different letters.' He paused, momentarily out of breath.

'It seems, Miss Grainger, that I shall have something to teach you.'

He sounded so like his father that I smiled and then remembered that he could not see me so I put out my hand and covered his. He did not move his hand away, nor did he make any sign that he had noticed the gesture.

'I hope we shall have a great deal to teach each other,' I said.

He nodded but went on as if I had not spoken.

'Father has had my school books printed in Braille for me but you can use the ordinary text books at the same time. I also have some story books in Braille. Perhaps I shall read you a story from them one day.'

I was made to feel that it would be a signal honour if he ever did.

That first morning in the schoolroom was more of a lesson for me than for him. I learned the Braille alphabet though I was unable to read as he did with his fingers. I found that it required a degree of sensitivity that I did not possess. I also discovered just how capable Alexander was. Not only was he an intelligent boy but he seemed to have overcome his handicap to a remarkable degree. Seeing him move around the schoolroom one would not have thought him blind, and I told myself that he must know the layout of the schoolroom very well. I was to find, however, that he moved just as confidently through every part of the house. It was only when I looked at his eyes, at the emptiness there, that I knew for certain that he could not see. I also was to discover what a retentive memory he had for the spoken word. Touch, hearing, all his other senses seemed to be heightened as if to compensate for his blindness. I discovered how sensitive his hearing was when he looked up and said,

'We have a visitor.'

It was some moments before I heard the footsteps on the stairs and I stood up as Lachlan Grant came in. He smiled at his son though he did not touch him and before he spoke Alexander said,

'Good morning, Father,' and his smile was a transformation. Gone was the small adult and in its place an eight-year-old boy at a schoolroom table. I found myself wishing he would smile like that for me.

'Good morning, Alexander,' said his father, 'I hope you are being helpful to your new governess.'

The smile disappeared and at once Alexander's face resumed its accustomed gravity. He did not speak.

'Alexander has been showing me his Braille books.' I said. 'I find them fascinating.'

'Not daunting?' There was a hint of a smile in his eyes and I smiled in return,

'A little perhaps and I'm afraid I shall never be able to read from them. But interesting nonetheless.'

'Then I hope that you continue to find it interesting, Miss Grainger. Older women than you have found the task too great. Is that not true, Alexander?'

The boy still said nothing and his father continued,

'But perhaps Miss Grainger is different?'

Alexander raised his head and appeared to stare out of the window. It was uncanny how difficult it was at times to believe he was blind.

'We shall see,' he said.

I was left to wonder why those other governesses had indeed left. Was it because the duties were so difficult or the child so remote, or was it as Araminta had said and they fell victim to the charms of Charles or his brother? Looking at him I could not imagine anyone falling in love with Lachlan Grant. Oh, he was handsome enough but there was a coldness about him that I found unattractive. My feelings for Charles I put from my mind for the moment. I was recalled to myself by my employer's voice. He asked if I had everything I needed to which I replied that I found the schoolroom extremely well-equipped and after some discussion of Alexander's hours of work and leisure he left with a brief word to his son which again produced that brilliant and fleeting smile.

The rest of the morning passed without incident and though I could not pretend that I had made any great progress with my charge I was not entirely dissatisfied with my morning's work. Alexander was to lunch with his father that day and I arranged to meet him in the rose garden after the rest that Dorcas insisted on him taking in the early afternoon. After a solitary luncheon in my sitting room I went in search of Charles. I found him in the library poring over some papers and looking unutterably bored.

'Felicia!' he cried, his face lighting up. 'Have you come to take me away from all this?' And he indicated a jumbled mass of papers on the desk and ran a hand through his hair as he did so.

I smiled in spite of myself. 'All what?' I asked.

'This,' he said and swept his arm in an arc over the papers dislodging a pile of them so that they floated to the floor like leaves in autumn. He groaned and sank back in his chair whilst I began to pick them up.

'What are they?' I said, glancing through them as I did so.

'They are millstones round my neck,' he said solemnly and I laughed.

'Accounts,' he continued, 'receipts, estate papers, I don't know. All I know is I have to get them in some kind of order for Lachlan. Don't you feel sorry for me?' He got up and started to walk towards me, his face a picture of misery. I suddenly saw exactly how he must have looked as a small boy.

'If they are duties then they must be done,' I said.

He staggered back in mock amazement.

'Spoken like a true governess. Oh, Felicia, beautiful Felicia, have I brought you here only to turn you into a dull school marm? Say it is not true.'

He reached for my hands but I avoided him. 'If it were it would be no more than you deserve,' I said.

He looked so forlorn that I relented.

'Oh, come along,' I said, 'we'll get them sorted out.'

It took the best part of an hour to sort the papers into their various groupings and enter the relevant figures in the ledger, and by the time we'd finished Charles was looking at me in admiration.

'You are the most extraordinary person,' he said, 'I had no idea you were such a business-woman.'

'I've always had a head for figures,' I said, 'and I enjoy organising things.'

'Better and better,' he said. 'From now on you can be my assistant.'

I looked at him severely and he immediately became woeful.

'I'm no good at it. I can calculate odds with no trouble at all but when it comes to rows of figures and accounts . . . '

I shook my head in despair.

'I don't understand why you're doing it,' I said. 'You don't seem to be the type to be handling things like this.'

He got up and strode towards the window, thrusting his hands deep in his pockets.

'Because Lachlan says I must,' he said, 'and in this house what Lachlan says is law.'

He sounded unlike himself, bitter, and I went on, 'But why must you do as he says?'

He ruffled his hair once more and when he turned back he was his old self again.

'Because Lachlan holds the purse-strings,' he said, 'and all you see around you is his. I am only the poor relation.'

I was puzzled. 'But you are his brother.'

'His half brother,' he corrected me, coming closer.

'But surely . . . ' I began.

'Oh, it is all too complicated,' he said, 'dull legal business about entails and suchlike. I don't understand it myself. All I know is that I am dependent on him and must work for my keep.'

I was indignant.

'But surely, Charles, it is most unbusinesslike of you not to know or even care about your position. It does not seem possible that one brother can have all this and the other nothing.'

He was standing over me and his eyes were smiling into mine.

'But I am not in the least businesslike, am I Felicia, or I would not have abducted you and brought you home with me? Do you mind so much that I have not a penny in the world?'

His hand came up and touched my hair, playing with a stray tendril and I felt my head swim. Then his words sank in and I drew back.

'And that is exactly why I have come to see you,' I said. 'Why did you bring me here under false pretences? You forged that letter from your brother, didn't you?'

He spread his hands in mock horror.

'Forged?' he repeated. 'Hardly that. It was harmless enough and I knew that Lachlan would see you for the paragon you are just as soon as you walked into the house. And besides, without that letter you would not have come.'

'You could have written to him,' I said. 'You could have asked him to interview me.'

He shrugged.

'Lachlan does not trust my judgement,' he said. 'He would merely have informed me that he would find someone himself, some horrid old harridan smelling of mothballs and with a permanent cold in the head and a moustache. Not my beautiful Felicia.'

I laughed in spite of myself at the vision he had conjured up, then I remembered the other reason I had wanted to see him.

'Why did you not tell me about Alexander?' I said.

'What about Alexander?'

'Oh, Charles, don't be obtuse. Why didn't you tell me the child was blind?'

He looked at me quite seriously and said, 'You might not have come.'

I felt myself flushing, torn between pleasure at his desire to see me here and anger at his fecklessness. Into my mind came the picture of myself on the very edge of despair and the strong arms that had pulled me back to life. He hadn't been feckless then.

'Charles, you really are the most irritating man,' I said.

He whooped with delight.

'You're not angry. Dear, adorable, Felicia.' And he grasped me round the waist and started to waltz me round the room. It was at that moment that Lachlan Grant walked in.

His look was cold as he surveyed us from the doorway and my face flamed as I tried to pin up the hair that had been loosed from its pins as we whirled around the room.

'My son is waiting in the rose garden,' he said.

That was all, but in his look was not only cold reproof — for a moment I thought I saw disappointment.

'I beg your pardon,' I said, 'I had no idea it was so late.'

The estate business must have taken much longer than I thought.

'Felicia was helping me with the papers,' said Charles, and I realised his arm was still round me. I moved towards the door as Lachlan, raising an eyebrow, said,

'Indeed?' in a tone that clearly betrayed disbelief, and moved aside to let me pass.

I hurried to the rose garden and though thereafter I regularly helped Charles with his papers, I always made sure I was on time for my duties.

Throughout those first weeks Alexander proved an interesting companion. He showed me the house whose history he knew in detail and I found the subject utterly absorbing; and if it sounds strange to say that a blind child 'showed' me the house, then I quickly found it perfectly normal. There were times, increasing as the weeks went on, when I truly forgot his blindness but I could make no progress in my attempts at friendship. He remained as he had been at the start — unfailingly polite, diligent and distant. Of his father I saw very little, though he made a habit of calling me to the library once a week to discuss Alexander's progress. At first I dreaded these occasions but gradually I began to enjoy them. He was an interesting man, well-read and with a dry sense of humour that I found confusing when it was directed at me as it sometimes was. When he relaxed he could be a most entertaining companion but there was always an undercurrent of tension about him even in his lightest moments. Charles was far easier to be with. We would go for rides together though he had to teach me to ride first, which he did very well. He loved horses as did Araminta. She would often join us and we ranged far and wide across the countryside, sometimes calling in on the Sutherlands at Greenholm Manor. I learned to love the Border country on these excursions and Alexander's stories lived for me as we rode the sites of past battles.

Araminta was a source of constant amazement to me. I began to admire her as a creature of absolute perfection in one respect — her self-interest. I had never met anyone who could so completely alter factual circumstances to suit her view of the world. In those days however it was Dorcas who troubled me most. She guarded Alexander with a fierce kind of pride that could be touching, if a little frightening. I was careful never to assume responsibility in her province. I asked her about the accident but she was not forthcoming. She pursed up her lips in an expression that I was beginning to recognise and said,

' 'Tis best forgotten. No good will come of dredging that up, and besides I thought the Master had spoken to ye of it?'

'He has,' I said, 'but you are his nurse and I thought you could tell me more about how it has affected him.' Her look was discouraging as I finished lamely, 'He seems such a reserved child.'

'Better that than the other way,' she said. 'I've nursed two tyrants in this house and that's enough for any family.'

I was surprised. 'You mean . . . ?'

She nodded, and I thought I saw a glint of pride in her eye as she said,

'Aye, ye wouldna think it now, would ye, but those two were the very devil. The one so fair and angelic looking but with a wayward streak in him that got him into many a scrape, and the other as dark as the devil himself and with a temper to match. It's a wonder murder was never done in this house when they were young. Aye, the laddie's better off as he is.'

And with that I had to be satisfied, though I found it hard to imagine the cool Lachlan Grant letting his temper get the better of him.

The house I continued to find fascinating. The oldest part was the Keep and Alexander was full of stories of its stormy past when the Border Reivers had fought over land that was now Scotland, now England. The rest of the house was something of a jumble, having been added to down the years in the various styles of the period, but it was to the Keep that Alexander and I kept returning. Though he would not go in when I asked to see where the animals had been kept and where the people had lived.

'It's unsafe after the spring floods,' he said, but I had the distinct impression that it was not that which kept him out of the Keep. I did not press the point for I was gaining his confidence slowly and that was too precious to me to risk losing. I had also begun to wonder about Vida. There was as yet no word of her homecoming and I found myself trying to imagine what she was like. Alexander never spoke of her. I had tried asking Charles and Araminta but their replies were unhelpful.

'To tell the truth,' said Charles with that engaging lop-sided grin of his, 'I wasn't here very much after Lachlan was married, or before come to that,' he continued, rubbing his chin, and I thought of the animosity between the brothers that Dorcas had described. 'Anyway, I came up for the wedding and she was certainly a stunner. Lachlan was mad about her.' He paused and looked thoughtful. 'Last time I was here things had changed a lot. I never knew Vida very well and she was certainly as striking as ever but Lachlan — well, I suppose that's what marriage does to people.'

I ignored his teasing look. 'You mean he wasn't in love with her any longer?'

He looked at me casually.

'You could say that,' he said, 'but why are we talking about boring old Lachlan, Felicia my lovely when there are so many more interesting things to talk about?'

'Like what?' I said.

'Like you and me.' And I laughed and the conversation resumed its normal bantering tone, but not before I said,

'Charles, was that after the accident, the last time you saw her?'

'Mmm,' he said, tucking back a strand of my ever-unruly hair. 'What is it about you, Felicia? Is it the hair that won't stay in its pins or the eyes that look so enquiringly on the world — or is it the governess in you that I find so absorbing?'

I had become used to his flirting and answered him in the same vein. I sometimes wondered if I were becoming too fond of Charles for my own good. He was charming and amusing but I never could tell when he was being serious.

I tackled Araminta on the subject of Vida as she sat in my room one day decrying my clothes.

'Felicia, you really must do something about your wardrobe,' she said, carelessly tossing one of my better day gowns on the bed. It slid to the floor and lay there, a crumpled heap of grey-blue muslin.

'Araminta, I'm a governess,' I replied, picking it up and trying to smooth out the creases, 'and governesses do not have 'wardrobes'; they have clothes.'

She pouted.

'Oh, don't be so dull. You're not a real governess.'

This was Araminta's constant cry, and indeed I was not treated as a governess in the house except by its Master, who behaved at all times with punctilious regard for my station. I had mixed feelings about that for while I appreciated the friendship of Charles and the camaraderie that Araminta showed towards me, the sort I thought wryly that she would display towards a plainer older sister, I nevertheless was beginning to take a pride in my work as governess to Alexander and both Charles and Araminta were too liable to forget that I had duties and expect me to be as free as they to go off on jaunts whenever it suited them. So I ignored her statement that I was not a 'real governess'.

'My clothes are perfectly adequate for my needs,' I said, then, as she turned her pretty face up to me and grimaced as if in pain, I too laughed for it had sounded too prim.

'You'll have to have something new for my eighteenth birthday ball,' she said. 'I'm not having you come in that boring old grey silk that you wear to dinner nearly every evening. Gosh, it's dull, Felicia. I'd almost rather you wore one of your parlourmaid's dresses than that.'

I had to agree with her though it was not the gown that was dull but me wearing it. I still could not put it on without thinking of that awful night in the Larkins' gaming room and I knew that, whereas before then it had suited me and the colour had reflected rainbows in my eyes, now when I wore it it was as if the gown itself drained me of colour and life. Still, it was the only one I had that was remotely suitable for the Dryford dinner table and there was nothing I could do about it.

'It will have to do, Araminta,' I said severely and was a little surprised to find that I had ssumed that I would be a guest. I wondered briefly if Lachlan Grant would object but I thought not. He probably would not notice.

'It won't,' said Araminta, her colour mounting, 'I'll find something for you. I'd force you to get something yourself if I thought you wouldn't appear in . . . in black bombazine,' she finished.

I laughed. She really was still very much a child.

'We'll see,' I said and a thought struck me. 'Araminta, will Mrs Grant be home for the ball?'

'Vida?' she said in a puzzled voice. 'I don't know, I hadn't thought. I'll ask Lachlan, or no, on second thoughts I don't think I will.'

She looked suddenly serious and it was so unusual for her that I said, 'Why not?'

'Oh, I don't think he likes her very much,' she said, offhand again.

'But I thought you said it was a wild romance . . . Venice and the gondolas and the moonlight?'

She crumpled my best shawl between her fingers and watched it expand again as she opened her hand.

'That was before,' she said darkly.

'Before the accident?' I said.

'Yes.' She cast the shawl aside. 'I was at school until last year,' she went on, 'so I hardly knew Vida, but I do know Lachlan and he's changed.'

Her small face was pugnacious. She sprang to her feet.

'Anyway married people always get like that after a while,' she said authoritatively, unconsciously echoing Charles. 'I'm going for a ride. Will you come?'

I shook my head. 'Alexander and I have work to do this afternoon,' I said.

She snorted and I reproved her.

'If you're not careful you really will turn into a governess,' she said, as she swept through the door. 'I shall go and find Charles. He's always fun.'

Yes, he is I thought to myself after she had gone. Then I began to wonder. Was it Vida who had changed or Lachlan and what was she like? I gave myself a shake. I was becoming obsessed with this unknown woman, but the afternoon's events did nothing to dampen that obsession.

Alexander and I went for our usual afternoon walk, and as often happened our path took us towards the Keep. I enjoyed these walks with Alexander. He was so diligent in the schoolroom that it was difficult to get him to chatter; but out in the open he relaxed, became more of a child though still somewhat distant. I often thought he worked so hard to make up for his disability, though I knew that he was already farther advanced in his studies than most children his age. I suspected too that he wanted to impress his father whose visits to the schoolroom, though more frequent of late, were still something of an occasion and Alexander loved to show him how well he was progressing. His father on his last visit had seemed particularly pleased and after a word with his son drew me aside. He looked at the boy's dark head bent in concentration as his fingers moved deftly over the thick embossed page,

'I have much to thank you for, Miss Grainger,' he said.

I was surprised. 'He is a remarkably intelligent boy,' I replied, 'and teaching him is a pleasure. Indeed on many occasions he has taught me.'

His eyes rested on me and I felt a tightening in my throat. This would be how Alexander's eyes would look if he could see.

'I was not referring to his scholastic progress,' Lachlan said gently. 'I do not think you realise how much happier Alexander has been since you came.'

I was touched and curiously proud. 'I would be more pleased than I could say if I thought that were true,' I said.

He smiled then, and the smile was so like Alexander's that I felt my breath catch and once again thought that the warmth that was in his eyes should but for that terrible accident have been in his son's. He took my hand in his and I felt the warm dry pressure of his fingers as he said,

'It is true. Miss Grainger, believe me, and please accept my apologies if I have been a little hard on you. Charles showed more good sense than I gave him credit for in bringing you here, even if the circumstances were a little unusual.'

I felt the colour mount in my cheeks and I released my hand from his. I would not tell him that I too had been misled. It would be disloyal to Charles.

'You are fond of my brother, I think,' he said. His eyes were fixed on me and I flushed even more.

'He was very kind to me. He . . . he did me a great service.'

One eyebrow rose in surprise and I realised that he had no knowledge of my first meeting with Charles.

'Indeed,' he said, 'then you have amply repaid that debt to our family. One thing only, Miss Grainger. You are young. Do not confuse gratitude with love.'

He said a final word to Alexander and was gone before I could reply, if indeed I could have found the words. My cheeks were hot with shame. He had quite politely but definitely put me in my place as a servant to his family and the warmth for him, the first that I had felt since coming to Keep Dryford, was gone as quickly as it had come.

As I walked towards the Keep with Alexander that sunny afternoon I felt again the sense of outrage that had enveloped me at his interference. He had virtually warned me off. Was I then just another of that line of governesses whom Araminta had described and, more important, was I in love with Charles?

* * *

So immersed was I in my recollections that I did not at first hear Alexander's voice.

'Listen,' he was saying. 'Do you hear it?'

'What?' I said.

We had come almost to the Keep and were standing on the low bridge that led into it. The Keep was closer to the river than the rest of the house and some Grant in the last century had had a channel dug so that water flowed from the river and around the tower like a moat before flowing back through an underground culvert to the river. It was a pretty idea but impractical, for the culvert kept choking and having to be cleared, something that I knew annoyed old Redpath who had to do it each time there was a heavy fall of rain.

I strained my ears, listening, expecting to hear an unusual bird song. Alexander loved all animals except horses and could identify birds by their call.

'I can hear nothing unusual,' I said, 'only birdsong.' He tutted impatiently and I looked at him in surprise. He was usually so calm.

'You must hear it, you must! It sounds as if it's in pain.'

I listened again but still I could hear nothing. His hearing was so much better than mine. Then all of a sudden he had darted away from me towards the door of the Keep. As he reached it his face became pale and I saw him shiver though the afternoon was warm and sunny.

'Alexander,' I said in concern as I reached him. He was standing in front of the heavy wooden door, his face white and set.

'It's in there,' he said, 'and I can't . . . I can't . . . ' He began to tremble violently and I put my arms round him.

'Alexander, what's in there? Why are you afraid?'

He turned his face to me and I searched for enlightenment in those clear blank eyes,

'You must come with me,' he said and he clutched the sleeve of my gown and then my hand. 'Please.'

I knelt beside him. I had never seen him afraid before.

'I'll come,' I said, 'don't be afraid.'

I tugged at the heavy wooden door and it opened onto a low hall. There were steps leading up and a door at the far end. He went immediately to this door, clutching my hand still, and it was then that I began to hear the tiniest of sounds. I opened the door then drew back in alarm, clutching Alexander to me. But he must have remembered from previous visits for his foot was already searching for the first step. The sound was louder now, a pitiful whining and scraping and in his eagerness he let go of my hand and plunged down the stairway towards it. It was pitch black in the cellar and I called out to him to be careful before I remembered that darkness meant nothing to him. It was some moments before I reached him and my eyes began to grow accustomed to the dark. I heard rustlings and whimpering and then an excited bark.

'Alexander,' I called, 'where are you?'

My hands felt around the walls. They were rough and clammy with damp.

'Over here,' came his voice. 'It's a little dog and it's hurt.'

I moved towards him as best I could, stumbling on the uneven earth floor. I almost fell over them. I knelt and felt with my hands, so much clumsier than Alexander, until I found a soft warm  bundle of fur. It whimpered again and made a feeble attempt to snap at my fingers, then my hands encountered a warm sticky patch and matted hair.

'We must get it out of here,' I said to Alexander. 'I will carry it, you lead the way.'

So Alexander led the way in the darkness while I followed behind, clutching the tiny bundle of fur to me.

Once in the hallway Alexander was triumphant.

'I told you I heard something. I rescued it. Oh, can I keep it?'

I looked at the animation in the child's face and at the disreputable little terrier that lay in my arms. Blood was dripping down my skirt from a freshly-opened wound, but on balance the dog did not look too bad.

'We'll need to bind it up,' I said. 'It must have cut itself trying to get free of that tangle of wire.'

I looked towards the stone stairway that led upwards from the hall. 'What's up there?' I said.

When I turned back his face was so pale that I thought he would faint. He seemed to be struggling with himself, then the dog whimpered again. He put his hand out to it and a small pink tongue came out and licked his fingers.

'I'll show you,' he said.

I followed him up the spiral staircase, hardly knowing what to expect. It was a circular room, the window slits set at intervals round the wall so that it commanded a view of the entire countryside surrounding the Keep. It was barely but beautifully furnished with rugs on the floor and a few pieces of fine old furniture. In one of the windows stood a tapestry frame with a stool before it. Alexander moved with a sure step to a chest shaped to the curve of the wall.

'In here,' he said, 'you will find cloth to bandage it.'

I laid the little dog in his arms and opened the chest. Inside was layer upon layer of folded, beautifully worked linen. I took a large napkin from the top and carefully bound it round the terrier's wound. It had almost stopped bleeding already and the animal was showing signs of recovery. I felt in my pocket for the sweet biscuits I habitually carried on our walks, for Alexander had a healthy appetite, and gave them to the child. The dog gobbled them up greedily as he fed them to it. I looked with interest around the room. Facing me on a low easel was a life-sized portrait of a woman. She was dark with slanting eyes and a sweet expression and I knew I was looking at Vida. I cast a glance at Alexander. His face was composed once more and he was absorbed in preventing the dog, which now seemed fully recovered, from jumping out of his arms.

'Alexander,' I said, 'this painting . . . '

His grasp on the dog relaxed and the animal bounded to the floor but Alexander seemed hardly to notice. He nodded silently then said with difficulty, 'This was her place, her special place.'

I went over and put my arms around him. 'And it will be again when she comes home.'

There was no expression on the pale set face and I found that more disturbing than anything as he said, in a cold little voice, 'She will never come home.'

Then there was the sound of a table being overturned and I turned to find the little dog grinning and wagging his tail delightedly in the middle of the debris. It was a small worktable beautifully made and inlaid with marquetry in an ornate style, and the contents of the drawers had spilled out over the floor.

'Oh, you naughty dog!' I cried, fearful that the table had been damaged. He looked at me and the tail slowly stopped wagging and drooped pitifully. I could not help but smile, then he was off again racing round the room excitedly. I looked in despair from the prancing dog to the debris of silks and bobbins and scraps of material that littered the floor.

'Alexander, we must find something to use as a lead for that animal or we will never get him home.'

'Don't call him 'that animal',' said Alexander, his little face pugnacious. 'He's just glad to be free again. It must have been frightening for him down there.'

I relented. 'You're right,' I said, 'and he's still a puppy. Look, we'll use this cord as a lead.'

The walls were hung with heavy curtains, presumably to dispel the chill of the stone and these were looped back with cords from the windows. I unfastened one and carefully tied a loop in one end and slipped it, not without difficulty, over the dog's head.

'There,' I said, 'now you take him downstairs while I tidy this up.'

I pointed Alexander in the direction of the stairs and watched them go, hoping that the puppy would not trip him up on the winding stone staircase. I sighed as I began to pick up the contents of the table and set it to rights. Alexander was so independent and that made it all the stranger that he should have been so afraid to enter the Keep. One thing I knew and that was that I would get nowhere by asking him the reason for his fear. I should have to find out some other way. I closed the last drawer of the table and sat back on my heels. 'She will never come home' he had said. I looked at the portrait, such a calm gentle face.

'Please come home,' I whispered to it, then there was a shout from below.

'Miss Grainger, come quickly. He's got away.'

As I made to rise something rustled beneath my skirt, a scrap of paper crumpled up into a ball. I thrust it into my pocket as I dashed for the door,

'I'm coming!' I called.

It took quite a time to catch the dog and I insisted that Alexander carry him the rest of the way home, no matter how much he struggled. As luck would have it we ran straight into Lachlan  Grant, dressed in riding jacket and breeches and looking, I noticed, very handsome. We came to a halt and the terrier leapt out of Alexander's arms and began to wrap its makeshift lead round my skirts, barking with excitement. He raised an eyebrow. I looked down to check the dog and for the first time became aware of my grubby skirts. My hands flew to my hair but it was beyond redemption. I don't think there could have been a pin left in it.

'Good afternoon, Mr Grant,' I said in as dignified a manner as I could, then Alexander was speaking, his face taut with apprehension.

'Oh, Father, we found a little dog. It was caught in the cellar under the Keep but it wasn't hurt, well not badly hurt and it really is very well behaved,' and I saw him cross his fingers behind his back, 'and can I keep it? Please say I can. I rescued it. Well, Flissy helped . . . '

'Flissy?' said his father and the eyebrow rose even higher.

I was too surprised to speak. Alexander had never called me anything but 'Miss Grainger' before. The child coloured slightly.

'It's what I call her,' he said.

'And does Miss Grainger approve of this new name?' said his father, but his eyes were on me and there was more than a hint of amusement in them. Alexander opened his mouth to speak but I intercepted him.

'Indeed I take it as an honour that Alexander has a special name for me,' I said firmly.

Alexander said nothing but put his hand in mine.

'So,' said his father, 'and must we all call her 'Flissy' now?' The amusement was unconcealed, and I blushed.

'No indeed,' said Alexander heatedly, 'it's my name for her.'

'So be it,' said his father, 'though at the moment 'Flissy' would seem to suit her better than Miss Grainger.' He was taking in every detail of my dishevelled appearance. He looked at the dog.

'That animal, Alexander, is only marginally more dirty than you. I suggest that you bathe and change while I take it to the stables. We will meet in the library when you have done so.'

I noticed that Alexander did not take issue with his father for calling the dog 'that animal' but nodded meekly. I also presumed that his remarks were also addressed to me.

I handed Alexander over to Dorcas, who was appalled.

'What have ye done to him, the puir wee laddie? Would ye just look at him. Whatever will his father say?'

'He's said it,' I said unsympathetically and she looked at me, scandalised.

'He's seen him like this?'

I nodded and she pursed up her mouth in the way that I was becoming familiar with.

'Call yerself a governess,' she muttered as she led the child away.

I do, I thought ruefully as I made my way to my own room, but no one else in this house seems to.

The mirror was no comfort! My face was flushed and there was a long muddy streak down one cheek. My gown was dirty and torn in places, and my hair lay about my shoulders in a tumbled mass of unruly waves. I rang for hot water and began to divest myself of the object that had once been a gown. It was ruined and I found myself thinking of the woman who had sat at her tapestry in the window of the Keep like some medieval lady. I thought of her calm face and sweet expression. She would never have got herself into this state, I told myself angrily as I kicked the bedraggled dress to the far end of the room. Dorcas was quite right. Governesses simply did not behave like this.

When Alexander and I appeared in the library I was dressed in my severest dark blue cotton and my hair was scraped back rigorously into a tight bun. Alexander was shining with cleanliness. His father made no comment on our appearance. It was decided that enquiries would be put in hand to see if the owner of the dog could be found. Alexander's face fell but his father pointed out that since it had no collar it was quite probable that the dog was a stray. I felt quite sure then that Alexander would not be disappointed and I smiled my thanks at him. He looked at me, his head on one side.

'Then I'm not such an ogre after all, Miss Grainger?' he said.

I blushed and was angry with myself. Really, it was becoming a habit. I made some excuse and left, taking Alexander with me, but I distinctly heard him say as the door closed behind us, 'Flissy!'

And I swear I heard him chuckle.

* * *

The finding of the dog marked a watershed in my relations with Alexander. He continued to call me Flissy and lost the gravity that had sat so strangely on a child. He became almost mischievous at times but I loved to hear him laugh and allowed him much more freedom than I would otherwise have done. I could not bear to think of him reverting to the pale polite little stranger he had been. For the same reason I did not mention the Tower Room to him but I determined to pay another visit to the Keep on my own. I did so a few days later. I had finished writing my weekly letter to the Larkins and had just put it in the box in the hall for collection. The house was quiet. Alexander was having his nap, though that rule was becoming more difficult to apply since the arrival of the dog. He had called it Fergus and it was his constant companion, even in the schoolroom, though Dorcas would not allow it in his bedroom.

As I mounted the spiral stair I knew that more than anything else I wanted to gaze again on that portrait and to wonder about the woman who had spent so much time here. I had asked Dorcas about that.

'The mistress used to go there near every day,' she told me. 'She said it was her quiet time and none was allowed to disturb her, not even the Master himself. She was that gentle. She used to make pictures of her home in her tapestries, her real home that is, in Italy. Ach, the poor wee thing, she missed it that much.'

'But was she not happy here?' I said.

'She was happy enough,' said Dorcas. 'She was happy with Mr Grant. It was just the difference. She was used to the sun, ye see, coming from foreign parts as she did. 'Dorcas,' she would say, 'when I work at my pictures I can feel the sun, smell the olive groves and it warms me in this cold land'. And what an olive grove might look like I don't know but it did her good to go up to that room on her own for a while.'

Yes, I thought, it must have been very different here for Vida. Even I felt it. Here the sky seemed to stretch for miles and if the air was cooler it also seemed purer somehow and free. I did not yearn for the home of my childhood or for the bustle of London. I loved this place and I realised then that I never wanted to leave it.

'I remember when she first took to going to the Keep,' Dorcas was saying. 'It was when she was carrying the child, and her no more than a child herself at the time. The Master had it all done just as she wanted it with the wall hangings and the furniture specially imported for her. She was that pleased,' Dorcas sighed. 'Aye but things change, nothing stays the same for long. I can picture her in my mind weaving those little scenes on her tapestry that reminded her of home.' And Dorcas stopped, clearly distressed.

I put my hand on hers comfortingly. 'And she will again when she returns, Dorcas.'

She looked at me and her eyes seemed to burn as she said,

'That she'll not. She never will again. That room hasn't known her this past year nor ever will.'

I caught my breath. It was what Alexander had said. 'You mean since the accident?' I said.

Her eyes glittered as she said, 'The accident, aye since the accident.'

The door of the Tower Room was open and I was about to enter when I stopped, for I was not alone in the Keep. Standing in front of the portrait was Lachlan Grant and on his face was a look of such tenderness that it was almost painful to watch. I drew back, conscious of intruding on something very private and quietly I went down the stairs and out of the Keep. He had not heard me. I doubt if he was hearing anything. He was alone in the room with Vida. I was conscious of a dull ache in my breast but I dismissed it. I was not ready at that time to face the truth.

# 4

It was on the afternoon of the ball that I found out that there was something wrong with the accounts. I had found myself with some unexpected free time. Alexander had been taken into the nearby market town of Greenholm by his father, mainly to keep him from getting under the servants' feet as they prepared the house for the ball.

I had been in the habit of helping Charles with the accounts once or twice a week but recently I had let this duty slide a little. Alexander was no longer taking his afternoon nap. He had successfully rebelled and even Dorcas was forced to admit that perhaps he was a little too old for such things, so he and I had been spending every afternoon together for the past few weeks and Charles had been left to get on with the work alone. Charles was often away on estate business but he had come home the week before for the ball. My time being so occupied with Alexander, I had found little oppor- tunity to be with him and he in turn had spent much of his free time with Araminta riding, sometimes with the Sutherlands and sometimes alone. When I did see him at dinner I had noticed a change in him. He was not his usual light-hearted self. I taxed him with it one evening.

'Duty is a hard burden to bear,' he said with his lop-sided smile.

'Poor Charles,' I said, 'you're not really cut out for it, are you?' But I felt that he was more troubled than I had ever seen him.

I was alone in the library. I had escaped there since it seemed to be the only place that was not being turned upside down. Everywhere smelled of soap and polish and great armfuls of flowers and potted plants were being brought in to decorate the house, much to the disgust of old Redpath who seemed to think that since they had been nurtured in the gardens and the conservatory that was where they should stay. I turned the pages of the ledger checking the figures against the pile of papers that lay beside me. At first I did not quite realise what I was looking at and then as I turned more pages I began to see that figures had been altered here and there. This was no faulty arithmetic. It was quite deliberate I was sure, though cleverly done, a nought here and there in the outgoings and in such an estate there were many outgoings. I sat there frowning. I must speak to Charles about this, I thought; then the door burst open and Araminta flung herself into the room and onto a chair.

'Well I've got it,' she announced.

'Got what?' I said, 'and please don't sprawl like that Araminta.'

'A gown,' she said, sitting up and twitching her skirts into place, 'for you . . . for the ball.'

I looked at her in amazement. 'What do you mean? I shall wear my grey silk.'

'You'll do no such thing,' she said sharply. 'This is my ball and you are not to come to it like some little mouse of a governess out of a novelette, and besides it's a perfectly splendid gown and it would be a pity to waste it. It won't fit me.'

'How do you know it will fit me?' I said.

She smiled like a kitten that had got at the cream.

'You remember the gown you ruined the day you found Fergus?'

I nodded.

'I stole it,' she said.

'Stole it?' I repeated.

'And took it to Miss Machivor who was making mine.' She stopped suddenly and rummaged in her pocket. 'Oh and I found this in the pocket. It must be yours. It's in French I think.'

I caught the scrap of paper as she tossed it to me and glanced at it quickly. My first thought was to remonstrate with Araminta, whose education must have been scanty in the extreme if she could not tell the difference between French and Italian, and then a curious feeling of excitement welled-up in me as I realised that it was the piece of paper that I had picked up in the Tower Room and that the words written on it in an overly ornate hand had been written by Vida. Once more I put it in the pocket of my gown as Araminta continued to speak.

' . . . and I chose the pattern and the material and, oh Felicia it is the most beautiful thing and she made it exactly the same size as that old parlourmaid's dress and I shall be so cross if you don't wear it.'

'That 'old parlourmaid's dress' was one of my better afternoon gowns,' I told her with some asperity, then I softened as I saw the tears standing in her eyes. 'Oh, very well, I'll wear it.'

A thought struck me. 'Araminta who will pay for this gown?'

'Oh, you don't have to worry about that. I've fixed it.'

'What do you mean, 'fixed it'?'

Her eyes shifted warily. 'It's coming out of my dress allowance.'

'Oh, Araminta, shame on you. You know you've spent more than your dress allowance this year already. I've just been going over the ledgers and you're far in excess of it and besides, you told me yourself your own ballgown was to be the last this year.'

She jumped up and stamped her foot.

'Felicia, you are the most boring, priggish, fussy old frump I've ever met and it's my birthday,' she wailed. She flung herself out of the door.

'And you'll probably be an old maid,' she finished.

She's probably right, I thought as I watched the door crash behind her. After all I was only two years older than she was and I was behaving like a dowager. The door rocked on its hinges as she thrust her head back round it. Her face was wreathed in smiles.

'Well, come on,' she said.

I got up and followed her, sighing. She really was the most changeable of creatures.

It was draped across the bed in my room and even I gasped when I saw it. I lifted a fold of the silk chiffon and let it slip from my fingers. Light as thistle-down, it floated for a moment before it settled. It was a deep red, not ruby nor claret but deeper than that, the colour of those roses whose velvety petals seem almost black in places and indeed when I lifted it the folds of the gown shadowed into soft darkness. It was the loveliest thing I had ever seen. I held it up to me and moved towards the looking glass.

'Araminta, it's beautiful,' I breathed.

'You see, you will wear it. You can't resist it.'

'Oh, I'll wear it,' I said, my eyes shining back at me from the mirror, then my practical good sense reasserted itself. 'It must have cost a great deal.'

Araminta shrugged.

'Not as much as mine. Wait till you see it. It's heavenly.'

I was looking at the gown more closely now, taking in the detail. 'Araminta isn't it cut rather low?'

She nodded absently. 'Yes,' she said, 'I told her it was for an older woman.'

I whirled round. 'I'm only two years older than you.'

She looked momentarily taken aback, then shrugged again.

'Are you? You seem older.' And I suppose that to her I did.

'Think yourself lucky then,' she was saying, 'I couldn't get Miss Machivor to budge an inch below here,' and she placed her hand just above her breasts. 'It's positively sick making and I'm sure it wouldn't happen in London. You could always tuck something into the top but I wouldn't bother if I were you. It always looks so obvious, as if you've got a mole or a wart or something you want to hide.'

I laughed and laying down the dress went across the kissed her.

'Thank you, Araminta, you are very kind.'

She looked at me, clearly puzzled.

'I'm not, you know, but I do want everyone to look pretty at my ball. I don't want to be a rose amongst thorns. I want to be a rose amongst . . . dahlias or chrysanthemums.'

I laughed. 'You mean you want a little competition.'

'Well, you must admit,' she said seriously, 'it's much better to be the most beautiful woman than the only one.'

'As I'm sure you will be,' I said.

She nodded complacently.

'I daresay I will. Now come and see my gown.'

I extracted the piece of paper from my pocket later that evening but I could make nothing of it. My Italian was scanty in the extreme and the handwriting would have defeated me on a cursory glance even if the language had not. Not only that but excitement at the thought of the ball and the gown I was to wear was beginning to rise in me so I put the paper away in my little jewel box and promised myself that I would begin to decipher it next day with the help of a dictionary. When at last I was dressed to go downstairs I couldn't believe that the vision that looked back from the mirror was me. Since my escapade with Alexander and Fergus I had scraped my hair back more conscientiously than ever but tonight I brushed it till it shone as softly dark as the shadows in the gown and looped it loosely high on the back of my head so that it fell in soft curls to the nape of my neck. Around my throat I wore the only piece of jewellery I possessed, a simple necklace of seed pearls and garnets that had been my mother's, and my shoulders rose white and smooth from the bodice of the gown. It was not quite as low as I had feared so I did not have to 'tuck something in' as Araminta had suggested but it was easily the most daring thing I had ever worn. I did not care however for when I moved it floated about me like gossamer and as I watched myself in the candlelit looking-glass I knew that I was beautiful. My eyes looked back at me and they had taken a dark glow from the gown  and I was happy. I made my way downstairs and as I descended the staircase Charles turned and saw me. His eyes moved over me and I accepted the expression in them as my due.

'Felicia,' he said as I approached him, then there was a rustle of silk on the stairs above us and Araminta was coming down on the arm of her guardian. She was in palest blue starred with tiny flowers that sparkled as she moved, and around her neck was a diamond drop pendant that struck sparks of blue and yellow and pink and green from its depths. Her hair was curled and interlaced with silver ribbon. She was the picture of youthful beauty. She fingered the diamond at her throat as she came near and looked up at Lachlan Grant, her eyes sparkling almost as much as the jewel.

'My birthday present from Lachlan. Isn't it beautiful?'

'Not as beautiful as you,' said Charles gallantly and bent to kiss her hand, his eyes dancing with merriment. I was surprised to see a faint blush rise in her cheeks as his fair head bent over her hand and something of this must have shown in my face for I felt Lachlan Grant's eyes on me and turned to find him regarding me somewhat quizzically.

'My brother is fond of paying compliments,' he said softly.

'And you are not,' I said.

'I told you once before that we Grants were never courtiers. The fewer compliments a man pays the more valuable they are,' he said smoothly. 'Allow me to pay tribute to your gown, Miss Grainger; it is very becoming.'

'It was a gift,' I said somewhat shortly, 'and I am very grateful for it.'

'Ah, gratitude again. You must get out of this unhealthy habit of being grateful, Miss Grainger. It ill becomes a beautiful woman.'

He was teasing me and I knew it, but I could not for the life of me answer as lightly.

'On the contrary, Mr Grant, I find that gratitude is one of the noblest of virtues.'

His eyebrows rose maddeningly.

'I see that the governess is not entirely absent even tonight,' he said.

'Oh, Lachlan stop baiting Felicia,' interrupted Araminta, 'you'll only frighten her away and she already thinks her gown's too daring for decency. Come along, Charles. You can take me in.'

I could not meet his eyes but I could imagine the amusement in them as he offered me his arm, remarking after Araminta's retreating back, 'Miss Grainger is nothing if not decent.'

I had perforce to dance the first dance with him though by rights it should have been Araminta, but I kept our conversation to the minimum and made my excuses as soon as the music finished.

'You have your duties to your guests,' I said.

'Of whom you are one,' he replied. 'I hope that you will allow me to partner you later this evening.'

I could not refuse. I was rescued by Douglas Sutherland. He seemed even quieter than usual but I did not much wish for conversation in any event. The ballroom was crowded with people laughing and talking and dancing. After our dance he said,

'Would you care to sit out for a while?'

I looked at him gratefully. 'I would indeed.'

He installed me at a little table set in an alcove and brought me some iced lemonade. As he sat down I followed his eyes and noticed that he was watching Charles and Araminta as they whirled about the room, their steps matching with easy grace. A thought took root in my mind.

'Araminta is looking very lovely tonight,' I said.

'When does she not?' he asked and his face looked so glum that it was almost comical. I felt I must tread carefully. I said tentatively,

'She and Charles look well together.'

He turned to me, his expression concerned.

'You have noticed. Forgive me, it must hurt you as it does me.'

I was taken aback by his sudden confidences. He had never been a man of many words and our conversations in the past had been only on the most trivial of subjects. He was speaking again.

'I have been much concerned over the past few weeks. I do not know if Lachlan realises.'

'Realises what?' I said stupidly. He looked at me in concern.

'You must know surely that Araminta and Charles have been very much in each other's company of late.'

'I know that they have gone riding a lot together, and also with you and your sister.'

'Not so often with us,' he said, shaking his head. 'I do not think Lachlan can know or he would be more anxious.'

'But why?' I said, 'Surely nothing could be more natural than for Araminta and Charles to be friends?'

'Friends yes,' he replied, 'but I am very much afraid that Araminta is falling in love with Charles. She is young of course and headstrong and he I suppose is attractive to women.' He stopped and coloured. 'I'm sorry,' he said, 'this must be painful for you.'

I looked at him in dismay. 'No,' I said, 'it isn't painful at all.'

'But I thought . . . '

I heard myself saying,

'So did I,' then I stopped. How could I tell a man I hardly knew that I had fallen in and out of love within the space of a few weeks?

'I see I was mistaken,' he said, 'forgive me. We thought . . . '

'We?'

'My sister and I . . . we thought . . . ' he stopped again.

'I understand,' I said, 'and please there is no need to apologise again. You may be assured that what you thought is not true.'

He looked unduly elated at this. 'I'm glad,' he said.

It crossed my mind that he might be glad for the same reason that Lachlan Grant would be. It was not suitable for a family servant, even a governess, even a hybrid between governess and friend like me, to be in love with a member of the family. Then I looked at him and realised he was too kind to entertain such a thought. His eyes were once more on Araminta and Charles.

'Why would Mr Grant not be pleased?' I said.

He hesitated.

'Charles is light minded and he and Araminta together . . . can you imagine? And besides, Araminta is heiress to a considerable fortune.'

I found myself suddenly furious.

'Are you suggesting that Charles would marry Araminta for her money?'

I might be no longer in love with him if indeed I ever really was, but I still regarded him with considerable affection.

Douglas seemed oblivious to my fury.

'Well, he has none of his own.'

'And whose fault is that?' I said.

'Fault?' said Douglas. 'Why his father's of course. He lost it and Charles has nothing.'

'But his brother . . . ' I began.

'Lachlan has been good to him of course, in fact some would say he has been too generous, especially in the paying-off of those last gambling debts. But it is to be hoped that now he is being made to work for the estate he will improve.'

My mind was whirling. Charles had said something about an entail and boring legal matters. Of course if the estate had come down through their mother . . . oh it was too complicated.

'You mean that all this belongs to Lachlan?'

Douglas looked shocked.

'Oh no indeed. The estate should of course belong to him entirely as elder brother but he has made half of it over to Charles. It's the money that runs it that belongs to Lachlan, through his father. Charles has no money, merely rights in the estate and that due to the fair-mindedness of his brother.'

117

'So Charles should have an interest in running the estate?'

Douglas gave a short laugh.

'If you mean a financial interest yes he should, but I'm afraid Charles's father left a good deal of debt so that only now is it beginning to show a profit. As for an interest in its affairs then Charles up until now has never shown much of that. That's why I mentioned Araminta's fortune.'

I was angry again. 'I think you misjudge him,' I said.

He smiled ruefully.

'Perhaps I do. In this case I am hardly the best judge.'

He was watching Araminta and his eyes were so sad that I regretted my sharp words.

'You are in love with her,' I said.

He bent his head.

'I daresay you think it's stupid. I'm more than ten years older than her but yes I'm in love with her and have been since she was in the schoolroom, and she needs someone older, someone who can handle her moods.'

Quite suddenly I recognised the man behind the mild exterior and I thought that if ever Araminta had the sense to realise it she would meet her match in Douglas Sutherland.

I looked up to find Lachlan Grant standing over me.

'Miss Grainger,' he said formally, 'might I have the pleasure of dancing with you once more?'

I walked calmly with him to the centre of the floor and when we began to dance I found the sensation of being in his arms strangely disturbing. I could not bear his silence.

'Araminta is looking very beautiful this evening, is she not Mr Grant?' I said.

He cast a brief glance in her direction and said almost dismissively,

'Pretty, I should say. I have other ideas of beauty.'

His meaning was unmistakeable and I felt myself flush as he continued, 'And why not call me Lachlan or do you detest the name? Then I could call you Felicia, or even Flissy if you prefer.'

'I hardly think that would be proper, Mr Grant,' I said firmly. 'I am after all in the position of a servant in your household.'

He laughed down at me.

'There you go again. You are quite determined to maintain your lowly status, aren't you? I could call that a form of snobbery.'

'You may call it what you wish,' I said. 'It does not alter the facts.'

'Ah, facts. You would of course be interested in facts. And what if I were to say that I found you curiously disturbing, Miss Grainger? What would you make of that fact?'

'Curiously disturbing can mean many things, Mr Grant,' I replied, 'and I would hardly call an opinion a fact.'

'Still the governess, eh? Well, let's see if I can improve on 'curiously disturbing'. How about damnably attractive, or strikingly beautiful, or desirable or tantalising or just plain maddening? Would any of these do? You may take your pick. They are all facts, or should I say opinions?'

'Mr Grant, I find your behaviour most incorrect and I must ask you to stop this nonsense at once.'

'Most incorrect,' he repeated. 'I do believe you have a gift for governessing. But incorrect as my behaviour might be, it is not nearly so incorrect as my feelings — now what do you make of that?'

The bantering note had left his voice and I was forced to look at him. I looked away again quickly for I felt he could see right through me.

'This is most unwise, Mr Grant,' I said. 'Your observations are improper to say the least and would be so even if you were free to make them.'

He hesitated momentarily in the dance and his arm gripped my waist almost fiercely as he drew me closer forcing me to look up at him. His eyes glittered and I could not read them as he said, almost under his breath,

'And there's the rub, Miss Grainger, I am not free.'

Fear twisted sharply in me at the emptiness in his voice then, mercifully as I thought at the time, there was a stir by the door. Lachlan looked towards it and grew quite still. His hand tightened on mine and I would have cried out in pain if I had not been looking at his face. He had gone completely white and his eyes were on the figure that stood in the doorway. I shivered at the thought of those eyes looking at me like that and turned to see more clearly. She was dressed in black and her dark eyes slanted slightly upwards in a smooth oval face. She saw him and began to move towards us. She seemed to glide more than walk and her gown rustled about her like leaves in autumn. For a brief moment I was reminded of childhood fairy-tales and I thought, the wicked witch has come to the ball. Then the moment was gone, a trick of the light that was all, and Lachlan said one word only and that on a strangely pleading note,

'Vida.'

She was beside us, her dark eyes turned up to him.

'You did not expect me, my dear?' Her voice was soft and slightly accented. She turned her eyes on me and once again I felt an inexplicable chill of fear as she said,

'And who is this delightful creature, Lachlan? I don't believe we have met.'

Araminta and Charles were at my elbow.

'Allow me to introduce Miss Grainger, the new governess,' said Lachlan.

Her smile did not falter but her voice was mocking as she said,

'A governess. Really darling, you could be a little more original, and in a gown like that.' Her eyes swept over me and I felt my cheeks flame, then Araminta's voice came high and bell-like.

'Do you like it, Vida? It was my idea. I chose it.' She was speaking wildly, trying to cope with the tension that hung in the air between Lachlan and his wife. 'At least Lachlan deserves some credit too, after all he paid for it.'

She faltered to a stop as Lachlan turned on her a look of cold fury while Vida said with a slow smile,

'Indeed? How very generous of him.'

I felt the hot colour drain from my face and my body was cold as ice. I was humiliated beyond all description, I felt someone take my arm and lead me away and then I was in the little parlour which led from the ballroom, while Charles stood over me with a glass of something golden. He held it to my lips and the fiery liquid burned my throat as it went down but I began to feel the cold leave my body and the shivering lessened.

I spent the rest of the evening with Charles. He was so kind.

'Don't upset yourself, Felicia. Vida was tired. She has had a long journey.'

'But Charles, she thought . . . '

'Nonsense, she only said that to hurt Lachlan. No one would believe such a thing.'

Eventually I was able to regain my composure and return to the ballroom. Neither Lachlan nor Vida were there and I was glad. Araminta came rushing up, her face flushed.

'I say, Charles, did you know she was coming back tonight? Lachlan didn't. He looked as if he could murder her. I've never seen him so angry, and with me too.' Her pretty face was torn between excitement and apprehension.

'Where are they?' said Charles.

She shrugged.

'They've gone. They went upstairs almost immediately and I haven't seen them since.

What a thing to happen. The way she looked at you, Felicia . . . '

I winced and felt Charles's hand steady on my arm.

'Come and dance with me, Charles,' said Araminta.

Charles looked at her in disbelief.

'I don't think so, Araminta. Felicia is still a little shaken.'

Araminta looked at him petulantly. 'But, Charles, it's my ball.'

Charles seemed to lose patience.

'Araminta, you are eighteen and yet you insist on behaving like a spoilt child. Why you haven't even apologised to Felicia for that stupid remark.'

She seemed genuinely surprised.

'But it was true. Lachlan did pay for the gown. He told me to make sure she had something decent to wear.'

I swayed slightly on my feet and Charles's hand steadied me once more. His voice was low and cutting as he said,

'Araminta, one day I shall get truly angry with you. Now go before you say anything worse.'

She made to speak then changed her mind as Douglas appeared at her elbow. She smiled brilliantly up at him.

'Well at least you won't be cross with me, will you, Douglas? Charles has grown quite stuffy you know.' And she shot me an accusing look before she went spinning across the floor in a swirl of blue and gold as Douglas looked down at her in wonder.

'She's such a child still,' said Charles, his eyes following them.

'I know, Charles,' I said, 'please go and dance. I don't want to keep you from your guests.'

But he wouldn't and we spent the evening dancing or quietly talking until, pleading a headache, I retired early to my room.

I did not sleep. I wanted to leave, to pack my things and go before the house should awake but that was impossible when I thought of Alexander. Poor little Alexander caught up in such violence of feeling. I shivered as I thought of the looks that had passed between Lachlan Grant and his wife. 'You could have been a little more original' she had said. Was this what had changed the sweet-faced woman of the portrait into the cool mocking Mistress of Dryford I had met tonight? It was anger that saved me, anger at his gall in ordering Araminta to ensure that I had something decent to wear; anger that his wife should so readily jump to such a conclusion; but most of all anger that a child like Alexander should be a pawn in their game.

I paced the floor restlessly as if movement would release me from the turbulence of my thoughts. The wind was getting up and rain began to spatter against the window as I drew the heavy curtains to shut out the night, to shut me in with my thoughts. As I undressed for bed, I thought of the things he had said to me, and my cheeks flamed at the memory. How dared he? I cast the gown from me and it lay there on the floor, beautiful still in its dark softness. I had nothing to reproach myself with, I thought, slipping my most severe nightgown over my head in defiance of the unashamed luxury of the ball gown. My replies had been, in my own words, perfectly correct. The sight of his face as he said those words — 'I am not free' — flashed across my memory and I thrust it from me as I removed my mother's necklace and put it in my little jewel box. As I did so my hand touched the piece of paper I had thrust in there earlier in the day and I smoothed it out. It was as I have said in Italian, and in an unduly ornate hand at that, but my mind was in such turmoil that I was glad of something, some mental task, to occupy it.

At the inadequate little school that I had attended there had been a drawing master, a little Italian with sad eyes and a droopy moustache. I smiled at the recollection of the fresh lace collars and ribbons that had appeared amongst the mistresses every Tuesday morning. I was not much good at drawing but I was a good listener with a thirst for knowledge and he would often talk to me of his home and even taught me some scraps of Italian, mostly poetry or homely little phrases. Somewhere amongst my things I still had the little Italian dictionary he had given me when I left the school. I found it in the depths of my trunk and I sat down to make what I could of the writing.

It was barely readable and the ink was smudged in places. Some words were obliterated altogether as if it had been left out in the rain but that was hardly possible. There was a date at the top. It was a page torn out of a diary and written more than a year ago — just before Alexander and his mother went on that fateful trip to Italy. There were words I could not make out, try as I might. As it was it took more than an hour before I could piece together fragments of the writing. I sat back and looked at what I had translated.

*I am so afraid . . . I must go . . . my little Alexander . . . surely he is not in danger . . . I love him but I fear . . . I will take him with me . . .*

And then at the end, written in so heavy a hand that the paper was almost torn through,

*My God, forgive me for my suspicions . . .*

I sat back, too shocked even to think clearly. One thing I knew. It was not rain that had smudged the ink so badly. I could see, as clearly as if I had been present, Vida sitting at her little work-table writing in her diary and her tears fell on the page as she wrote. Of what was she afraid, or of whom? But I knew the answer, did I not? I had seen the look in his eyes as she stood in the doorway. Dorcas knew — the temper of the devil she had said, but I had seen him look at the portrait in the Tower Room. What terrible thing had happened that two people should change so much? And more importantly, what of Alexander, was he in danger?

It was like a physical compulsion. I knew it was madness but I could not help it. I had to go and see if Alexander was all right. I threw a shawl on over my nightgown and, swiftly, my bare feet making no noise on the thick carpet, I crept along the corridor to the boy's room. The wind was stronger now. I could hear it gusting distantly, making the old house creak and groan. Several times

128

my imagination got the better of me and I had to stop and listen, sure that I could hear someone moving around, but it was only the wind I told myself. I reached his door and listened, then I put my hand on the doorknob and turned it. It resisted and I pushed again. I was alarmed. Surely it could not be locked?

I thrust the weight of my body against it and it opened but some force seemed to be trying to close it against me. I pushed again and this time it opened fully and I found myself hanging onto the doorknob to save the door from crashing back on its hinges for the wind had caught it. I looked in disbelief at the open window while great gusts of wind surged into the room and threw sheets of rain at me. The curtains had been pulled roughly back, and billowed into the room. I threw myself at the window, sparing only a glance for the sleeping boy. The wind whipped at my shawl and the rain swept my hair in rats' tails across my face as I leaned out trying to catch hold of the windows which lay flattened against the outside walls. So insistent was the beat of the rain and so harsh in my ears the sound of the wind that I almost cried out when a strong hand reached out from behind and plucked me from the sill. In a matter of seconds he had the windows shut and the curtains drawn against the night. He turned to me, his hair plastered across his head like a close-fitting cap.

'I heard noises,' he said. 'What are you doing here?'

What could I say? Not 'I read your wife's diary and was afraid for Alexander'.

'I thought the wind might frighten him,' I lied, then I realised what I had found so odd. 'But he's sleeping soundly. How can he in this?'

Lachlan bent at once towards his son and I knelt by the bed.

'The counterpane is wet,' I said, then I saw the expression on his face. 'What is it?'

'Sleeping draught,' he said shortly, lifting Alexander's eyelids one by one.

He put his ear to the child's chest.

'He's breathing quite naturally. He'll be all right. I'll stay with him for the rest of the night.'

'You mean someone did this deliberately?'

His mouth was set in a grim line.

'Looks like it, doesn't it? You get to bed, and change out of those wet things before you do. You look like a drowned rat.'

I looked down. My nightgown clung to me and hastily I picked up the wet shawl and wrapped it round me.

'Modesty even at the risk of pneumonia,' he said with a trace of a smile. 'You're a wonderful girl, Felicia. Now get to bed.'

'You'll have to change the blankets,' I said, 'the counterpane is soaked through.'

'Yes, ma'am,' he said, and for the first time I noticed the tiredness around his eyes. I put out my hand to him.

'He'll be all right,' I said. 'He's very strong.'

He was turning once more towards his son.

'Bed,' he said roughly, and I went.

It was curious, I had gone suspecting that Alexander was in danger, suspecting moreover that that danger came from his father. I had found him in danger, for surely he would not have escaped serious illness exposed all night to the storm? I had found the person I had suspected on the spot and yet I did not now believe that it was from Lachlan Grant that the danger to Alexander threatened. I peeled off my wet things and put on a fresh nightgown. Was I a complete fool to trust him as I did? I had left him alone with the boy, but he was his father.

One thing had not changed however, I thought, as I drifted into sleep. And I swore to myself that the child would not suffer because of the almost tangible violence of feeling that existed between his parents.

# 5

I went to the schoolroom as usual next morning but it was fully an hour before Alexander arrived. By that time I had made up my mind to say nothing of the incident of the previous night. I thought I understood what had happened. Dorcas had obviously given the child a sleeping draught to save him being disturbed by the festivities, the window had been left slightly open on what had been a pleasant evening and with the arrival of Vida Dorcas had forgotten to come and close it when the rain began. It was the only reasonable explanation. To read anything more into it would be nonsense. And of course his father had been angry. Perhaps Dorcas had been acting against his wishes in giving the child a sleeping draught, certainly she had not told him. I would make no mention of it either to Alexander or his father. It could serve no useful purpose.

When Alexander arrived I was shocked at the change in him and my first thought was that he had taken harm from his exposure to the rain during the night, but then I saw that the cause of the change in him lay deeper than that. Gone was the happy, rosy-cheeked little boy that he had become and in its place was once again the small pale ghost of an adult.

'I apologise for being late,' he said stiffly, 'my Mama arrived unexpectedly last night and I was required to go straight to her this morning.'

I looked at him in dismay.

'That is quite all right, Alexander,' I said. 'Indeed if you wish I'm sure your father would not mind if we forgot about lessons for today. Your mother has been away for some time. You may wish to spend the day with her.'

The skin around his taut little lips whitened as he said, 'That will not be necessary.'

That was all, but the emptiness in his voice filled me with pain and an unreasoning anger that the progress we had made should be wiped out like this.

The events of the previous evening filled my mind, the things that Lachlan Grant had said to me, things that he had no right to say no matter how lightly; his wife's insinuations and the implication that the situation was not unusual. What were they doing to this child? I looked at him bending over his book, his fingers tracing out the words painstakingly and my heart went out to him. I thought once again of those dark slanting eyes and heard anew that softly accented voice, saw in my mind's eye the look on Lachlan Grant's face as he saw his wife. I pushed the thoughts away and concentrated on Alexander. By the end of the morning I was pleased to note that he had smiled several times and that the colour had returned in some measure to his cheeks, but as we prepared to go down to lunch he suddenly grasped my hand as I helped him replace his books.

'You will not go away, Flissy,' he said desperately, 'now that she is here?'

I looked at him in concern. His whole body was rigid with tension. I bent down and put my arms around him and he allowed me to do so.

'I will not go away, Alexander,' I promised.

He relaxed and his arms came round my neck in a swift hug, then he composed himself once more though he said,

'I think I shall take a nap after lunch today.'

'Very well,' I replied and arranged to meet him afterwards. As I made my way to my own room my mind was not wholly at rest. It had been some weeks since he had last taken a nap and I wondered what had prompted this return to what he had dismissed as a babyish habit.

I was summoned to the library after lunch. As I left my room I cast a last look at the box in which I had carefully packed the ball gown. It would not be an easy interview. He was seated at the desk, the light behind him so that I could not immediately see his face. He rose as I entered and motioned me to sit down.

'I feel I owe you an apology, Miss Grainger,' he began. 'My wife had only just arrived home after a long and arduous journey and I fear she was somewhat overwrought.'

I felt the colour mount in my cheeks as I replied,

'I understand, Mr Grant however, your wife was quite right in one respect. It was unseemly that I should be wearing a gown that you had paid for. Believe me if I had known I would never have accepted it from Araminta.'

'Araminta,' he said impatiently, 'I expressly told her not to mention to you where the money for the gown had come from.'

'You misunderstand,' I said more firmly than I would have believed possible. 'I do not blame Araminta.'

He looked directly at me and his face was pale against the blackness of his hair. 'Then you blame me?'

I took a deep breath. I may be dismissed for it, I thought, but I had to stand by my principles.

'I think it unsuitable for an employer to make a governess such a gift.'

'But you had no suitable ballgown.'

Humiliation stabbed painfully again.

'I have a perfectly adequate gown that suits my station in this house,' I replied, 'and if that were considered inappropriate then I need not have been invited to attend the ball.'

'And if I wanted to make you a gift?'

'It was an unsuitable gift,' I repeated.

He seemed to lose patience.

'Miss Grainger,' he said, 'I could not have cared less if you had attended the ball in riding breeches. You would have looked just as beautiful. I am a plain man and being a plain man I assumed that any young woman would have been pleased to have a new gown and besides, I wished to express my gratitude for what you have done for Alexander. It was a gift. Are you too proud to accept a gift, Miss Grainger?'

I remained stubbornly silent and his face darkened.

'Would you have accepted such a gift from Charles?' he said.

I was suddenly angry.

'You have no right to ask me such a question,' I cried. 'You are my employer, not my guardian.'

'I am well aware of that,' he said, 'but you are living in my house and I feel some responsibility for you.'

'I am well able to look after myself,' I said.

He rose and for a moment I thought he would come round the desk towards me but instead he merely placed his hands flat on its polished top and leaned towards me.

'Are you indeed?' he said. 'And what would you consider a suitable gift? A Latin primer perhaps?'

I lowered my eyes, determined not to be browbeaten.

'I have packed the gown in tissue paper and put it in a box in my room. Perhaps one of the maids could return it to Miss Machivor. It is possible that she might find a use for it amongst her usual customers.'

Out of the corner of my eye I saw him flinch and I thought I had gone too far, but he merely resumed his seat and when I looked up he was regarding me calmly once more.

'I see that I cannot persuade you to accept my gift?'

'No.'

'Very well,' he said. 'We will say no more about it.'

I made to rise but he stopped me. 'There is one thing more, Miss Grainger.'

He was playing with the pens in his tray.

'I find that I have to go away on family business. I very much hope that while I am away you will take full charge of Alexander. His improvement in the last weeks has been a source of considerable pleasure to me. I hope that you will continue to make progress with him.'

'I shall continue to do everything that I can for him,' I replied. 'But surely now that his mother is home . . . '

He did not let me finish but cast aside the pen he was toying with and rose from his seat. He moved towards the window and stood there looking out for a moment.

'I think I told you before that Alexander's relations with my wife are not as one might expect between mother and son,' he said carefully.

'But with time,' I said. 'They have seen so little of each other this last year.'

I stopped in confusion, for of course Alexander had not 'seen' in the proper sense of the word at all the last year. He turned towards me again.

'I see I shall have to speak plainly,' he said. 'Since the accident my wife has been greatly changed, a different person one might say.' His voice was low, as if he were speaking more to himself than to me. 'She is nervous and unpredictable and I have arranged for Dorcas to look after her. Dorcas will no longer have time to spare for Alexander.' His voice changed. It was urgent now and almost pleading as he came towards me, his eyes on my face. He stood looking down at me.

'You understand,' he said, 'Alexander will be in your care. Dorcas will be my wife's constant companion.'

He took my hands in his and his face was close to mine as he bent his head.

'Look after Alexander,' he said, 'I would not go away if I did not have to. Only look after the boy. If you should find yourself in need of help then go to Alison but remember this, I go only in the sure knowledge that you will be here.'

Then he released my hands and was gone from the room. I swayed on my feet, unable to comprehend the urgency of his words, caught up in a sea of whirling thoughts and emotions, only with the knowledge that I was no longer Alexander's governess but his protector. But his protector from what?

I did not see him before he left, only heard the clatter of his horse's hooves on the driveway later that afternoon, and I realised that I did not know where he had gone or even how long he would be away.

I was summoned once more just as I was going up to change for dinner, but this time it was Vida who had sent for me. She was in the small drawing room and I noticed that Dorcas was in attendance.

'Ah, the governess,' she said in her slightly accented voice as I entered, and two spots of colour burned high on her delicate cheekbones. I barely stopped myself from dropping a curtsey at her tone and stood quietly before her, my hands folded in front of me. She did not ask me to be seated. She was again all in black, a gown of the finest silk beaded with jet that seemed to quiver though she was sitting quite still. I realised that she was still in mourning for her sister though by this time she should surely be allowed a touch of colour. Black suited her and once again my mind compared her to some dark queen out of my childhood fairy-tales.

Her voice was imperious as she said, 'I understand you have been in the habit of dining with the family.'

It was not a question and I gave no answer.

'This is a practice that I consider quite unsuitable,' she continued. 'A good governess would never have consented to such a thing. However, since this is your first post I shall overlook it.' Her lips curved in the suggestion of a smile. 'Particularly since you have been regarded in rather a different light than as a governess in this household. I gather you were a friend of my brother-in-law, Charles, before you came here.' The smile was evident now and cruel. 'I would not wish you to presume on that friendship.'

I bit my lip and thought of Alexander. I must not antagonise her by replying.

'You will take your meals in your room from now on. You will soon learn what is expected of a governess.' She turned from me as she was speaking and picked up a piece of embroidery she had been working on.

'You may go,' she said.

I was dismissed. I had said nothing. I had accepted her insults and innuendoes and said nothing. Tears of anger stood in my eyes as I reached my room and I almost dashed the tray with its covered dishes from the table in my sitting room in my frustration, then I saw that the box containing the ball gown had gone and in its place was a small parcel. I opened it. It was a book of poetry and written on the flyleaf was 'I hope this is a more acceptable gift, Lachlan Grant'. All my anger disappeared and, touched by his thoughtfulness, I sat down to my solitary meal in a more docile mood than I would have believed possible.

I had barely finished eating when there was a tap at my door and Dorcas came into the room. With her was Alexander and behind them two maids with blankets and a footman with a truckle bed. I looked at them in wonder as they began to set the bed up under Dorcas's instructions but she motioned me to silence so I merely waited until they had finished and been dismissed. I put my arm around Alexander's thin shoulders.

'What is this about, Dorcas?'

'Master's orders,' she said shortly. 'The boy hasn't been sleeping well of late and Master thought it best if you were close at hand.'

'But that's nonsense,' I began, then I looked at the pale little face beside me and wondered if it were nonsense.

'May I have Fergus here?' he said to Dorcas.

She pursed up her lips then her eyes grew soft as she looked at him.

'Don't see why not if Miss Grainger don't mind,' she said.

'May I, Flissy, please?'

I was almost too surprised to reply. Dorcas had always been so set against Alexander having the dog in his room.

'Of course you can, Alexander,' I said.

I should have liked a private word with Dorcas but she had gone.

'They'll be finished dinner by now,' she had said. 'I won't wait any longer.'

I settled Aledander for the night in the sitting room and retired to my bedroom to read but I spent more time wondering what was going on than I did reading the book of poetry Lachlan had left for me, and when I at last fell asleep I was no nearer an answer.

All my time was now spent with Alexander and I hardly noticed how Araminta was avoiding me until I came across her cutting roses in the garden a few days later.

'Araminta,' I said, 'won't you come for a walk? Alexander and I are going down to the river.'

She looked up from her flower basket. 'I'm too busy,' she said.

I looked at her. 'Too busy for a walk and a chat?'

'I'm helping Vida with her flower arrangements,' she said and turned back to her work.

I shrugged and moved on, but I found it odd that she should prefer work, however pleasant, to a stroll and a gossip. She must be getting on very well with Vida and I supposed I should be glad. For myself I avoided the mistress of Dryford as much as I could, conscious nonetheless of how at times I would find myself looking up at a window and find her watching me. It made me shiver slightly and I was glad Alexander could not see her. He spoke rarely of her and only when asked a direct question and the subject caused him such distress that I avoided it whenever possible.

Charles was a different matter. He waylaid me one day on my way from my room to the schoolroom.

'I can hardly believe it,' he said. 'You're alone. Where are your shadows?'

I laughed.

'I only came to fetch a book I had forgotten. I'm just going back to them.'

He seized my hand. 'Come for a walk this afternoon.'

I laughed again. 'We'd love to.'

'Oh, not the circus. Just you, Felicia.'

I frowned. 'I can't, Charles. I have Alexander to look after.'

'But can't he sit with Dorcas or amuse himself or something, anything, for an hour?'

'No, he can't,' I said firmly. 'Dorcas has her duties to Mrs Grant now and I have mine to Alexander.'

'Duties. There you go again. I swear, Felicia, if you don't mend your ways you'll end up with a moustache and a dewdrop on the end of your nose like all the rest of your breed.'

I laughed once more and he gave in and agreed that we would all take a walk that afternoon.

'What's all this about Alexander moving into your room?' he said as we walked together towards the Keep at the appointed hour.

'He wasn't sleeping well,' I said glibly, 'and Dorcas thought he'd be better off with me in case he needed anything during the night.'

Charles grunted. 'Oh that's it is it?'

'Why?' I said. 'What did you think?'

His eyes laughed down at me and he pulled my arm through his as he said,

'I thought perhaps Lachlan had decided you needed a chaperone while he was away. He doesn't trust me you know.'

I couldn't take offence but his words struck a memory and reminded me of what I had been wanting to talk to him about.

'Charles,' I said carefully, 'have you been doing the accounts regularly since your brother left?'

I thought I detected a slight wariness in his look but he said pleasantly enough,

'Your devotion to duty has inspired me to heights of diligence quite foreign to my nature.'

I wouldn't be side-tracked. 'Have you noticed anything odd about the figures?' I said.

There was a definite wariness now.

'Odd?'

I looked at him. He was so obvious. 'Charles!'

He squeezed my hand, suddenly serious.

'It's all right. I'll put it back and he'll never notice.'

'But why, Charles?'

He let go of my hand and kicked moodily at a fallen branch.

'It was that last visit to London, the night I met you.' He looked at me carefully but I could think of that evening now with a curious calm.

'Go on,' I said.

'Well, I'd lost a packet and Lachlan had said that any more debts and I was out. No more allowance. No more home. No more anything. Don't you understand, Felicia? If he found out I'd be out on my ear. It was my last chance. Believe me, that night I knew exactly how you felt standing by the river. It could have been me.'

All my anger disappeared.

'It's still stealing, Charles,' I said gently.

He turned and his eyes, usually so good-natured, blazed with something near to fury.

'Stealing?' he said. 'From my own land? My own inheritance?'

'But, Charles,' I protested, remembering what Douglas had told me.

'Oh I know,' he interrupted, 'I know in law I have no real claim but even Lachlan recognises that I have a moral right. Can you imagine what it's like, Felicia, to be a younger son? Simply by an accident of birth to have no right in law to your own home. To be dependent on someone else's sense of fairness. If I had been the elder it would all have been mine. I wouldn't have to account to Lachlan for every penny I spend. I'd be free to do what I liked and instead I'm not. He's given me a share in the estate but I've got to work for it. All the money's tied-up. I've got to toe the line or I get nothing and just because my father was no good with money. But then I don't expect you to understand that.'

But I did. I understood so well, for if my own father hadn't been so unlucky my mother and I would never have had to leave our home. I touched his arm gently.

'I do understand, Charles. Really I do.'

He flashed me a look of wonder. 'By God, Felicia, I believe you do.'

He took my hands and bent his head to mine, then Alexander's voice could be heard from further along the path.

'Flissy, where are you?'

Charles turned and I could not see his eyes as he said,

'It'll all be his some day. Even my share. Lachlan will buy me out. I know he needn't and he'll be generous but it'll all belong to Alexander and he'll never see it again.'

I shivered as if a cold wind suddenly blew about me.

'Charles, don't say that.'

He turned, his old smiling self once again.

'Sorry, just being morbid, but the duns are after me and I always feel just the tiniest bit vulnerable when that happens.'

I drew in my breath. 'Debt collectors?' I said.

He nodded. 'The worst kind. You can't sue for gambling debts, you know. But don't you worry. I have a plan and if it comes off I'll never have to worry about money again.'

'Oh, Charles, not more gambling.'

He laughed and patted my hand.

'I suppose you could call it a gamble, but it's not gambling.'

Then Alexander's voice called more urgently and we made our way towards him.

That night I was awoken from a deep sleep. At first I did not know what had disturbed me, then I heard the low rumble of Fergus's growl. I was suddenly fully awake. Silently I crept from my bed and moved towards the open door of my sitting room. Alexander was deeply asleep, his cheek pillowed on his hand, his hair darker than ever in the moonlight that filtered through a crack in the curtains. Fergus was standing at the end of the bed, his ear cocked, the hairs on the back of his neck standing straight up.

As I watched the handle of the sitting room door turned silently and softly the door was opened. I caught a swift glimpse of a dark figure before Fergus began to bark then the figure disappeared as quickly as it had come and I was at the door throwing it wide, Fergus at my heels. I silenced him and peered into the darkness of the corridor in time to catch sight of the edge of a dark cloak or dressing-gown disappearing round the corner. I sped along to the turning but there was nothing to be seen. Whoever it was had gone. I returned silently to my room, soothed back to sleep a half-awake child, calmed the dog and sat for a long time before I, too, fell asleep. But before I did I made sure that both doors to the corridor were locked. I was glad of Fergus.

I looked with special interest at the household the next day. Who could it have been? Certainly no one who cared to be seen or they would not have fled when Fergus began to bark. No one made mention of the incident and in the circumstances neither did I. I did not want to be summoned by Vida and dismissed for having nocturnal visitors to my room. I had little chance to speculate however for that afternoon Araminta had hysterics. She had lost the diamond pendant Lachlan had given her for her eighteenth birthday. I tried to calm her but it was no good. The house was turned upside-down in an effort to find it. The diamond was not found. The gold chain on which it had hung, however, was. I was sent for by Vida and dismissed.

The interview with Vida was not pleasant. I made no answer, no defence to her accusations. It would have done me no good but I did wonder who had done this to me. All I could think of was that now there would be no one to look after Alexander and, as I remembered Lachlan's last words to me, my throat tightened in fear. When I left Vida to go and pack I ignored her orders and rushed straight upstairs to Alexander. He was alone.

'Alexander,' I began.

'I heard,' he said. His voice was small and I could see traces of tears on his cheeks.

'I did not take the diamond,' I said firmly.

He turned to me, his mouth curling scornfully. 'There was no need for you to tell me that.'

'I'm sorry,' I replied, 'I should have known you would not believe that of me. But I shall have to leave, Alexander.'

His head drooped. 'Like the others,' he said.

There was nothing I could say, no comfort I could give him for he was right and like the others I was leaving. I went to him and put my arms around his slight body. He clung to me and for a moment I thought — I will take him with me — then good sense told me that to add abduction to an accusation of theft would be an act of madness. I heard swift steps on the stairs and I whispered to him urgently,

'Alexander, be careful. Your father will be home soon but until then keep Fergus with you and take care.'

His beautiful sightless eyes were on my face and I gasped at the knowledge I seemed to see there.

'I'll be careful,' he said.

I wanted to probe more deeply, to ask him what he knew, but at that moment the door was flung open and a voice said,

'What the devil is going on?'

Alexander's face became its old polite mask again and I turned to Charles.

'You've heard?'

'I was out all morning. You're not leaving?'

'I must.'

'But it's absurd. No one would believe it.'

'Vida does and the chain was found in my room.'

'The chain,' he said dismissively. 'Anyone could have put that there. What about the diamond?'

'They haven't found that yet,' I said.

'But she can't send you away just because someone put the chain in your room.'

I became impatient.

'Oh, Charles, don't be obtuse. I'm a servant. It's a wonder I'm not being sent to prison.'

'But when they find the diamond,' he said.

'If they find it.'

'Oh they'll find it,' he said airily, 'You know Araminta. It'll probably be in her handkerchief drawer or somewhere but, Felicia, I shall miss you.'

I looked at him. Charming, debonair, and I wondered if I had been right in assuming that he had taken the diamond. It was a dreadful thing to think and I could not believe that he had deliberately implicated me, but he needed money so badly and only I knew why.

'And I shall miss you, Charles,' I said and it was true. 'And now I must go.'

I turned to Alexander and gave him a swift hug. There was nothing to say and I left him sitting on his own in the schoolroom as pale and withdrawn as when I had first met him. I sighed.

'Charles, will you take a letter to Alison for me?'

He looked surprised.

'Why, yes, of course, but if you want to see her she's here. We were out riding this morning.'

'Do you think she would come to my room? There isn't much time.'

He squeezed my hand. 'I'll tell her.'

There was a light tap on my door and Alison entered. She was wearing a dark blue riding habit that suited her delicate colouring and I noticed her cheeks were flushed.

'Felicia, my dear,' she said coming towards me, her hands outstretched. 'This is a terrible thing. How upset you must be.'

153

I nodded, but I could not waste time though I was grateful and touched by her sympathy.

'It's about Alexander,' I said. 'He will have no one to look after him now that Dorcas is needed by Mrs Grant.' I hesitated, unsure of how much to say. 'His father told me just before he left that if I should need help, if Alexander . . . ' I stopped. What could I say? 'Alexander is in danger. From what or from whom I do not know'. She laid a hand on my arm.

'I understand,' she said. 'Lachlan spoke to me too. I shall be here each day.'

I thanked her but at the back of my mind I was thinking, and what about the nights? What if someone comes again to his room? Lachlan had not known of that.

She was still speaking.

'When I met Charles out riding this morning and he told me the news I came at once for this very reason. I would do anything to help Lachlan and Alexander.'

I looked at her shining brown hair, her kind eyes, her sweet smile and I felt a sharp pain that she should take my place with Alexander; then I pushed the thought away as her words struck me.

'Charles told you?'

'Yes, he was coming back from Greenholm when we met. He must have left very early this morning. Still, it seems to have been worth it. He was in high spirits.'

Had he said he had only just heard or merely implied it? I could not remember.

There was a tap at the door and a maid stood there.

'The carriage is ready to take you to the station. Miss,' she said.

I stood up. 'I'm ready.' Then, turning once more to Alison, 'You will take care of him?'

She pressed my hand. 'I promise,' she said, 'and Lachlan will be back soon.'

'You have heard from him?'

She nodded.

'This morning. He expects to be back within the week.'

I felt a great sense of relief but it was tinged with anger. Only a few more days and Lachlan would have been home. Only a few days, but during those days Alexander would be here, alone.

And so I left Dryford Keep, my mind so occupied with thoughts of the child that the carriage was half-way to the station before I remembered that I had not seen Araminta; but surely Araminta would not believe that I had done such a thing? That was the irony of it all. No one seemed to believe that I had taken the pendant, no one but Vida. As the carriage trundled its way to the station the sky was low and threatening and when I alighted the first drops of rain began to fall.

'Aye, it's set for a storm,' said old Redpath. 'I've seen it before. It'll last for days more than likely.' And I thought how fitting it was that even the weather matched my mood.

*   *   *

Once again I was going to the only place I could. The Larkins were, as always, kindness itself. I did not tell them why I had been dismissed. It would have been too distressing for them, and they, to their credit, did not ask. Mrs Larkin only remarked,

'Why we got a letter from you only the other day and you said nothing of leaving.' Her kindly face was puckered in concern.

'The child's mother came home,' I said, 'and I was no longer required.'

It was not a lie. It was simply not the truth. She gave me a long look and pursed up her lips but I could not tell what conclusions she had drawn and I did not much care. My mind was going round in circles wondering who had implicated me. Who had put the gold chain in my room? Was it Vida? She had wanted rid of me from the moment she had set eyes on me, I knew that. But to go to such extremes. Then Charles's face swam into mind. He had a plan he had said only a few days before, a plan that would clear his debt — but he had also said that it would mean the end of his money worries for ever. One diamond pendant, no matter how valuable would not do that. Then in my mind's eye I saw him look at Alexander and heard his words, so bitter, 'all this will be his and he will never see it'. Alexander. I worried constantly about him but he was safe with Alison. She had told me she would do anything for Lachlan and I believed her. The thought came unbidden. Had she wanted me out of the way so much that she had thrown suspicion on me? I could not believe that. The faces swirled in my mind. Vida, Charles, Alison until I thought I would go mad then Mr Larkin's voice broke in.

'You know you're welcome here, my dear.'

I felt close to tears as I thanked him.

'I'll help in the hotel again,' I said. 'I must do something to earn my keep.'

Mrs Larkin clucked again,

'Now don't you think of such a thing after the kindness shown to us by your Ma and Pa.'

I did help in the hotel however, though I never set foot in the gaming room again. I had been there two days before I asked about my stepfather.

'He's been around a couple of times,' Mr Larkin said, 'but I can handle him, don't you worry.'

'He's been bothering you,' I said, feeling guilty.

He was silent for a moment,

'He's a strange creature. I'll speak quite plainly, my dear. That man hates you and if he can hurt you he will.'

He leaned across and took my hand.

'If ever he should come around and I'm not here you promise me you'll not let him in. If need be you bar the door, guests or no guests. You promise me now.'

I promised and a shiver of fear crept up my spine. Mr Larkin would not extract such a promise from me unless he felt it was necessary. After that I was on my guard. I would sometimes think I caught sight of him as I came back to the hotel after doing some errand for Mrs Larkin, then I would see that it was only a man in a black coat, a harmless stranger. If I did not take hold of myself I would become fanciful.

I had been there almost five days and was becoming obsessed with thoughts of Alexander. Was his father home? Was the child all right? I had left the hotel that morning to go to market. The little maid was turning the Larkins' room upside-down for they had gone to visit an aunt of Mrs Larkin's in the country who was sick, and would be gone all day. It was the perfect opportunity for a 'good turnout' as Mrs Larkin called it. I rounded the corner and again I noticed a black-coated figure. My heart began to beat painfully and I told myself I was imagining things. He was too far away to be identified. Then all thought of my stepfather was banished from my mind, for there entering the hotel was Lachlan Grant.

I stood rooted to the spot for a moment then a great joy filled me. He was back and I hardly knew how my feet carried me to the door of the hotel. He was there in the hallway holding out his card to the terrified maid of all work, who was standing quaking in front of him. His back was towards me and little Rose was saying,

' . . . to see Mrs Larkin's old aunt who's sick with her chest, sir.'

She saw me and relief flooded her little face.

'Oh here's Miss Felicia, sir, and she'll attend to you I'm sure.' And she fled.

He turned, the scrap of pasteboard fluttering to the floor, and with a shock I realised what had made Rose quake. I took a step backwards as the full force of his fury struck me like a blow.

'There are matters to be settled between us, Miss Grainger,' he said. 'Is there somewhere we could talk in private?'

I looked towards the parlour in confusion. It was in total disorder, buckets and brooms strewn around and the furniture in chaos.

'There is only my room,' I said diffidently, still shocked by his evident anger.

'Then that will do,' he said.

'But it is hardly proper,' I protested.

'There are more important things than propriety,' he said stonily, and stood aside to let me pass.

I led the way to the little room I had on the first floor and, as I mounted the stairs, so my anger mounted. What right had he to treat me this way?

He closed the door behind him and I turned to face him.

'You left him,' he said, and I almost reeled at the barely-contained fury in his voice.

'I was accused of theft.'

He waved a hand dismissively. 'No one believed that. You did not even protest your innocence.'

'I was a servant in your house. Does a servant protest innocence and expect to be believed?' My anger was beginning to match his.

'And had you been treated as a servant?' he asked.

'Since you left, yes.'

'By whom?'

'By your wife.'

Again that impatient gesture. 'You had friends in the house.'

Charles. How could I tell him that I suspected Charles of taking the diamond? Or his wife or Alison for that matter? I said carefully,

'If I had refused to take the blame someone else would have been implicated not only of stealing but of casting suspicion on me.'

'The diamond was not stolen,' he said shortly.

I felt as if I had been struck.

'What do you mean?'

It was as if the matter were of no importance to him.

'It was merely hidden and the chain put in your room to make it look as if it had been stolen.'

My head reeled. Then it had not been Charles. Who then? Vida? Alison?

'By whom?' I whispered.

'Araminta.'

I looked at him in disbelief. 'Araminta,' I repeated stupidly.

'She was jealous of you.'

'But why?' I was totally confused.

'It seems your relationship with Charles had given her cause,' he said with distaste. 'I believe it began to irritate her on the night of the ball.'

I sank onto the bed. My legs would not support me.

'But she has no cause to be jealous,' I said.

'I wish I could believe that,' he said.

I looked at him, anger rising in me once more.

'And why should you not believe it?' I asked.

He shrugged.

'This is beside the point. The point is that you left when I had trusted you, depended on you, to stay.'

I was on my feet again facing him.

'I had to go!' I cried. 'I was dismissed. I did as you asked. Alison is looking after Alexander. What more could I do? Surely you understand. You told me to go to Alison if I needed help.'

'It is not Alison that Alexander needs,' he said softly though his voice was still hard, 'it is you.'

I spread my hands in despair then my voice rang out.

'Your wife told me to go.'

His eyes had a strange light in them, then he said quite deliberately, 'She is not my wife.'

For a moment I took his words quite literally and felt myself sway on my feet, then my common sense reasserted itself and I looked at him coldly.

'Perhaps you do not live together as man and wife,' I said. 'It is certainly true that you do not behave towards each other as a man and wife should. If you did then Alexander would be a happier little boy; but she is still your wife . . . '

His hands were on my shoulders, shaking the breath out of me.

'Do you think I do not know how unhappy my son is? Do you think it does not torture me to see him so? But believe this, she is not my wife.'

I looked at him and believed. The floor tilted beneath me and at once his arms were all round, steadying me.

'Felicia, Felicia. I did not mean to tell you so abruptly. Forgive me.'

I reached out and touched his cheek with my hand.

'I do not understand,' I said, bewildered.

He ran a hand through his hair.

'I barely understand myself,' he said, 'all I know is that I came here today to tell you the truth, to bring you back to Dryford to Alexander and to me for ever, if you are willing to take us on.'

He smiled wryly and I smiled back.

'You have never given me cause to think . . . ' I began.

He interrupted me,

'I know, I know. I have been fighting against it ever since you came but I thought it was Charles that you loved and then when I came home and found out what had been going on, I spoke to Charles.' His eyes were on mine, searching. 'He said you were one of his few failures. Tell me it's true, Felicia.'

I laughed.

'It's true,' I said. 'It is not Charles that I love.' Then he was kissing me and all the hurt and bewilderment was gone. We drew apart and I said, 'But you must explain.'

'Later,' he said, 'on our way to Dryford. There is no time to be wasted.' He tilted my chin and his eyes were dark and impenetrable as he said,

'Will you trust me, Felicia? Will you come back to Dryford with me now and trust me?'

I shivered slightly at the note in his voice but I said,

'Yes, I will trust you.'

I hastily packed some things and left a note with Rose to give to the Larkins. In it I gave what explanation I could and promised to write more fully soon. Little Rose stood in the doorway, too frightened still of

Lachlan to speak. She muttered something to me as I came down, something about a guest, then Lachlan appeared with my bags and she stumbled to a halt. I did not know what she thought and I did not care for I was ablaze with happiness and it must have shown. It was not until we were ensconced in a first-class carriage, mercifully alone with the countryside flashing past the windows, that he turned to me and took my hands in his.

'And now I will explain,' he said.

# 6

His voice was low but clear as he began his story and a strange story it was too.

'You know of course that I met Vida in Italy, in Venice where she was staying with friends of her family. Her own family home was in the north of Italy. I was on the Grand Tour. I was young, no more than a boy and she was so sweet, so gentle and at the same time exotic, foreign, different from anyone I had ever known. I fell in love with her immediately, head over heels. She told me little of her family at first. It was as if there was some sorrow there that she could not bear to speak of. It was only after I had asked her to be my wife that she told me and asked me to accompany her home before she would give me an answer. That was when I met Carla. It was an extraordinary meeting. At first I thought I had gone quite mad. She was an exact replica of Vida, my Vida.'

His head dropped into his hands for a moment and I reached out to him but already he was speaking again.

'They were identical twins, she and her sister, but that was not the secret that weighed so heavily on Vida; oh no, it was much more than that. At first I did not notice and then odd little things began to strike me. Carla was rarely left alone. She did not go on visits to friends as Vida did. It was when I came across Vida in the garden one day, crying, that she finally told me. Carla had found out that Vida and I were planning to marry. Vida had a little pet bird that she loved, a finch I think it was. She had found it that morning dead in its cage. It was then, as I comforted her, that she told me what she had been afraid to tell me before, but by that time I was not unprepared for what she was to say.

'Carla was like her only in looks. In everything else they were as different as night and day. Carla was unstable. Her parents knew this and that was why she was kept at home. There had been other incidents like that of Vida's little bird. She was not mad, not raving, nothing like that — but she was a strange creature with moods and fancies and her hold over Vida both fascinated and frightened me. Vida was very fond of her sister. There was a bond between them, the kind of bond I believe only exists between identical twins. But they were so different, like light and dark, good and evil, two sides of the same coin. Vida was gentle, perhaps too gentle. It was as if her sister drew the energy from her and in her way Carla loved Vida. She could not bear anyone else to possess her, and so of course she hated me, for I was taking Vida away from her. I think it was the hardest thing that Vida ever did, to come away with me as my wife. Her guilt was terrible and I have never known till this day whether I did the right thing in insisting that we marry. But as I have said I was young and headstrong and very much in love, and to me it seemed ridiculous that a woman should not marry the man she loved for fear of upsetting her sister.

'That was how I looked at it then — upsetting Carla — but of course it was much more than that. Vida was never truly happy at Dryford. There were times when she would forget about Carla and then when Alexander was born I thought that surely now with a child of her own she would settle, but that was not to be. She loved me and doted on Alexander, but it was as if there was a thread that plucked constantly at her, a thread that bound her to Carla. I would come across her sometimes in the room I made for her in the Keep where she was at her happiest and it was as if only her body was there, her mind was far away in Italy with her sister.'

He stopped for a moment, lost in thought, and I made no move to speak for I too seemed to see her sitting at her window and stitching at her tapestry, thinking of the home she had left and Dorcas's words came back to me with all the implications that she had left unsaid — 'aye, she were happy enough with the Master'. He began to speak once more.

'It was because Carla hated me so much that Vida and Alexander went alone to Italy. She seemed to have some strange premonition for she clung to me the night before she left and made me promise that if ever anything should happen to her I would look after Carla at whatever cost. I remember her words 'we are so alike — but for an accident of birth it could have been me'. So you see, it was not Carla that was killed, it was Vida. My Vida.'

His voice was very low now and his eyes far away. 'I did not realise at first that it had not been an accident. By the time I got there my wife had been buried as Carla. I had been told that it was Carla who had been killed. I arrived to find Carla bordering on a state of madness. Her parents were terrified of what she might do. It seems that since she had killed her sister, and she had killed her quite deliberately, she had been unable to live with the knowledge. It was as if she had killed herself and I suppose that in a way she had, and so she became Vida. For all I know she may still believe she is Vida. All I know is that I arrived to find my wife dead, my son blind and Carla believing herself to be my wife. Her parents were elderly and very frightened. They could no longer cope, that much was obvious. I was hardly sane myself and over and over in my head I heard Vida's words as she asked me to look after Carla. It seemed to me at the time only right. In a way I felt myself to blame. If I had not taken Vida away, had not married her, none of it would have happened. There was only one thing to do, only one way to ensure that I should always have the care of Carla. I brought her home as my wife, as Vida, and she has never spoken the name Carla since.'

\*   \*   \*

He stopped and I reached out to him, 'But Alexander,' I whispered.

His face twisted in pain,

'Do you think I have not been tormented by that?' he said. 'Do you think I have not thought every day since of his seeing not his aunt but his mother killed?'

'Then he knows?'

He shook his head wearily.

'How can I tell? He knew at the time, that is certain but he put the memory of it from his mind as he put sight for ever from his eyes.'

I grasped his hands. 'But he does remember,' I protested.

He looked at me in wonder.

'He does,' I insisted, and went on to tell him of the afternoon in the Keep when he told me his mother would never come home.

'I thought he just did not believe that she would return, but I see now that he knew because he remembered her death.' I was leaning towards him, urging him to believe me and his face was slowly losing some of its pain.

'Then I was right to go,' he said. Then, more briskly, 'These last weeks I have been in Italy. No one could know where I had gone lest Carla find out. She hates Alexander almost as much as she does me. I was afraid for him but I had to go myself to obtain documents, statements from Vida's parents, proof that Carla is not my wife.'

I was puzzled. 'But why so suddenly?'

My hands were in his and his look turned my bones to water.

'Because of you,' he said. 'When she came back and I saw you together that evening of the ball I knew it was useless, that I could no longer fulfil my promise to Vida.'

171

'But you loved Vida still,' I said, my voice a whisper. 'I saw you in the Tower Room looking at her portrait. I did not understand until now how you could look at a portrait so and at the woman so differently.'

'I was saying goodbye to Vida that day,' he said. 'When I lost her I thought my life was over, that I would never love another woman, and then you came into my life.' He bent his head to my hands. 'Oh, Felicia, you have no idea how jealous I was of Charles.'

I raised his head and looked into his eyes and knew that all he said was true. 'There was no need,' I said.

He smiled a smile of such sweetness that I was momentarily startled at the resemblance to Alexander. His left eyebrow went up.

'No need at all?' he said.

'Well, only a little at the beginning,' I said wickedly.

'Flissy,' he said, as his mouth came down on mine.

Later I said to him 'Does Alison know all this?'

'She has always known,' he said. 'She was Vida's friend. That's why I told you to go to her if you needed help. I could not tell you the truth until I had been to Italy, until I had purged myself of the last year, until I was truly free.'

'And Dorcas?'

'Yes.'

'And why you went away?'

'Alison knows. I spoke to her about it. She has always been like a sister to me since we were children.'

I thought of Alison and her happiness that morning. What exactly had he told her? That he was going to be 'truly free' soon? Surely not that it was because of me that he craved his freedom. I looked at him. Did he not know that she was in love with him? But I said nothing.

# 7

It was almost midnight when we arrived at Dryford in the station pony-trap, and the household was asleep. Lachlan saw me to my room and we stood for a moment looking down at the sleeping form of his son.

'He did not want to go back to his own room,' Lachlan said.

I felt tears prick the back of my eyes.

'I will not leave him again,' I whispered. Lachlan turned then and his arms went round me.

'Nor me either,' he said then he bent and kissed me, not with passion as he had done earlier that day, but with a gentleness that was infinitely more affecting.

'Till the morning, my love,' he said and was gone.

I was there in the morning when Alexander awoke.

'Good morning,' I said gently.

His voice was uncertain. 'Flissy? Is it you?'

I went to him. 'Yes, it's me.'

He flung his arms round me, his face alight.

'You've come back.'

'For good this time,' I said.

'You mean it? You won't go away again.'

'Never.'

He sighed contentedly and I made a solemn vow to myself that never would I let him down again.

'Now then, breakfast, young man,' I said briskly to hide my own emotion. 'How have you been? Has Alison been to see you each day?'

'Oh yes, she's been very kind,' he said carefully, 'but it wasn't the same. I don't think Fergus liked her quite as much as you.'

I laughed and scolded him for using Fergus as an excuse.

'Let's see how Fergus enjoys working,' I said. 'I don't suppose you've been doing your lessons since I left, but it's work as usual today.'

He grinned and my heart lifted at the sight of him so boyish once more.

'We've had the most frightful storms,' he said. 'Thunder and lightning and the rain has been amazing. Redpath says the river has risen so much it threatens to burst its banks, and he's got rheumatism again.'

He chatted freely as he dressed and I looked out of the window. It had been too dark to see last night but the sky was heavy still with rain; and the river, so placid and shining in my memory, was now a turbulent muddy mass swift-moving and angry.

'Redpath says there's more to come,' Alexander said complacently.

'You weren't frightened?' I asked.

'Of thunder?' he scoffed. 'Not a bit. Fergus didn't like it much though. He woke me up growling the night before last but I gave him a biscuit and talked to him for a while and he was all right after that.'

My heart lurched uncomfortably and I hoped that it had only been the storm that had disturbed Fergus. I could not help it. I found myself saying, 'That was the night your father came home.'

'Yes,' said Alexander, 'and what a rage he got into when he discovered you'd gone. Dorcas said we were lucky murder wasn't done.'

Araminta came to my room whilst Alexander was at breakfast.

'Lachlan told me to come,' she said, scuffing her foot on the carpet like a naughty child come to apologise. 'I suppose you're absolutely wild,' she went on.

Curiously enough I found I was not even angry, 'Why don't you tell me about it, Araminta?' I said.

Tears welled-up in her blue eyes and sparkled on her lashes.

'I was so cross,' she said, 'you looked so beautiful at the ball, everyone said so. I know I wanted you to look nice but I didn't expect you to look quite as nice as that.'

I tried to suppress a smile as she looked accusingly at me from under her lashes.

'I'm sorry,' I said.

'Oh it wasn't your fault. I don't suppose you could help it.' At this I did smile and her eyes flashed at me warningly. 'Not in that gown at any rate,' she said, tossing her head. Then, 'But when I told Vida Lachlan had paid for it he was angry with me and Charles too and it was my ball and then Charles wouldn't even speak to me and if it hadn't been for Douglas I would have been utterly miserable and all because of you.' She stopped.

'Are you really in love with Charles?' I said gently, 'for you know there's only friendship between us, nothing more. You had no cause to be jealous.'

Once more her eyes flashed as she tossed her head.

'Charles,' she said scornfully. 'I really quite dislike Charles now. He's been positively hateful ever since he found out what I did and I didn't really mean to. It just sort of happened. I really did lose the pendant, you know, and Vida said you'd probably taken it for she'd seen the way you looked at it, just the way you looked at Charles she said, and then when I found it was in your room and I remembered being there last time I'd been wearing it and it seemed so easy just to take the diamond and leave the chain.'

All at once her face crumpled and she came and sat beside me. 'I'm truly sorry, Felicia,' she said miserably.

I put my arms round her. 'It's all right, Araminta. I'm not angry. I understand.'

And I did understand. Vida (or must I now call her Carla?), had worked cleverely on Araminta's imagined slights, on her little jealousies. She was at the root of it. And what else was she at the root of, I wondered. Then Araminta said, mopping her eyes.

'You're truly not cross?'

I smiled. She was such a child still. 'I'm not cross,' I said.

She gave a great sigh. 'Douglas said you wouldn't be but I didn't believe him. I would have been furious.'

'Douglas?' I said, amused.

She nodded.

'He was so kind when I told him what I had done, well I had to tell someone. Lachlan was coming home and I knew he would find out the truth and Douglas was so sweet and he wasn't cross at all and he told Lachlan for me. I couldn't have told Lachlan.'

I patted her hand.

'It's all over now and you don't have to worry about it any more,' I said. 'It's forgotten.'

She smiled up at me. It really was unfair that Nature had endowed her with the kind of face that could cry itself silly and still look so lovely. Her smile was like sunshine after rain. No wonder Douglas hadn't been 'cross'.

After lunch Alexander and I thought we'd take a walk. The sky was still threatening, but if we didn't go far we'd get our walk before the rain began again. Lachlan met us as we turned the corner of the house. Alexander was playing with Fergus a little way off. He looked at his son for a moment before taking my hands in his.

'I have to go into Greenholm', he said urgently, 'to see my lawyers and lodge the papers I brought from Italy with them.'

I nodded.

'I'll be back as soon as I can,' he said. 'I daren't leave the papers in the house.' His eyes were grave. 'Soon it will all be over, Felicia, I promise you.' And he bent swiftly and kissed me.

I watched him go round the house to the stable block and as he disappeared a shadow fell across me. I looked up and there, towering above me on her great black stallion, was Carla. There was no confusion in my mind as I looked into her eyes. This was not and had never been Lachlan's wife. I had not heard the horse's hooves on the wet grass and my thoughts betrayed me as my eyes went at once to Alexander. I saw her lips curl and she turned her mount without a word and set it to a gallop across the lawn, straight for the boy. The words froze in my throat but at that moment Fergus leapt more boisterously at his young master and they rolled together over the wet turf. The hooves of the great black horse pounded past, inches from them. Alexander's face turned towards the sound and I saw fear contort his features.

'Alexander,' I heard my voice, unnaturally calm. 'You'll catch cold if you roll about on the wet grass.' My calm transmitted itself to him and he rose and came towards me putting his hand in mine.

'Where shall we walk?' I said.

'To the Keep,' he replied at once. 'Redpath says the moat's really full now and I want you to paint the picture for me.'

It had become something of a game with us on our walks. Alexander would describe the calls of birds and make me listen for them and then he would say,

'Paint me the picture, Flissy,' and I would describe the scene in detail while he listened.

180

'We'll go to the river,' I said, 'but not to the Keep, not today. The culvert's choked and the foundations are unsafe.'

'Then the bridge near to the Keep, please Flissy.'

I agreed. It was extraordinary how drawn he was to that place and yet how unwilling to enter it.

We stood on the bridge and I leaned on the low parapet and watched in fascination the water below.

'It sounds like some great roaring beast,' said Alexander. 'I can imagine it's a dragon and not a river at all.'

'It's like a dragon,' I said, and described the torrent that poured under the bridge carrying with it the debris of the recent storms. The sticks and twisted branches hurtled past, submerging and re-emerging in its turbulent depths. At first I thought it was one of the sounds of the river but then I realised that it was not. It came again, a low laugh that chilled me to the bone. I turned to find Carla standing not a yard from me. She was still dressed in her black riding habit and her eyes glittered with the fire of insanity. But it was not that which caused me to tremble and caught the breath in my throat, for behind her was the black-suited figure of evil that had haunted me for so long. My stepfather. I felt all colour drain from my face and I was aware that I was shaking violently. The thought passed through my mind — was it I who was mad? Was this a ghost, a figment of my imagination? Carla laughed again.

'So it is true,' she said.

I opened my mouth but no words came. I stretched out my hand and felt Alexander's fingers close around it, warm and comforting.

'I met him in the stable yard,' she said, and the look she cast him was one of utter contempt. He stood there, his lips parted to show those pointed teeth, his hairy hands plucking at his coat. I could not tear my gaze away. I was once again a terrified child fascinated by this loathsome creature. Carla was speaking. Her words came to me distantly.

'He had a great deal to tell me. Of your mother and your life after you left his house. You did not tell us that you had such an interesting past, my dear, but of course I should have known that any friend of Charles would be bound to be interesting.' She made the word sound evil. 'It was clever of him to pass you off as a governess but a pity that you had to look further. Charles I should not have minded but Charles was not enough for you, was he? You had to have Lachlan too. What a lot of practise you must have had in that . . . what was it you called it, Mr Petheridge, 'hotel'?'

My lips were dry, my voice cracked. 'It's not true,' I whispered.

Again her laugh, but I was still watching him. He was mouthing words now and I did not need to hear them to know what they were. Flecks of foam flew from his lips and I watched, mesmerised, as they settled in his beard. His eyes were alive with hatred.

'Look at me,' she said suddenly and I was jerked as from a dream. Slowly I turned to her and I was not surprised to find her face so close to mine.

'And what do you think Lachlan will say when he hears of this? Has he told you that I am not his wife?'

My face must have shown some trace of emotion for her eyes snapped then narrowed.

'I see that he has,' she hissed, 'and you believed him. Yes, I can see you believed him. Tell me, my dear, does it sound likely? Would any man do what he claims to have done? There had been others before you, others who have left this house shamed and humiliated. Have you been shamed yet?' She brought her face even closer. 'But then it would not be a new experience for you, would it?'

'No, it's not true,' I repeated and then, for I could not help myself, I turned once more to him. 'How did you know? How did you find me?'

He spoke for the first time, and his voice struck me like a blow.

'He left his calling card, didn't he, when he came to see you. I waited, I waited a long time. I saw you leave. I picked up the card. I was on the same train, not in the First-Class, oh no, I had to make do with the Third but I suffered the journey gladly, do you hear, to catch up with you.'

My mind reeled. Rose and her mutterings about a guest. It had been no guest. It had been him, then the thought of him on the train, waiting, hating all the way. I could not bear to think of it. My hands came up to cover my face but Carla's hands were almost as quick. I looked deep into her eyes. They were black. There was no light in them anywhere.

'Slut,' she said and I felt her spittle on my face and flinched. 'Charles picked you up in some tawdry gambling den and you lured my husband back there. Slut.'

I was hypnotised. Her voice went on, unceasing, mesmeric — saying things I could not even understand and I found myself moving under her hands until I was standing by the parapet of the bridge and the water churned its murky, chaotic way beneath me.

'You almost did it once before, didn't you? I know your story. I know all about you. Do you think he'll have you now, even as his mistress?'

I was barely listening to her. All I could feel was despair. Was she not right? Had he lied to me? Was she indeed his wife? Had my love for him blinded me to all reason? I felt the pressure of a hand on my back. This time, this time, I thought. She murmured words. They came to me low and clear and they were not English words but I understood them. I felt myself sway and the water rose and fell before me, then the world was full of light and in my ears a roar as of a great beast waiting, but above it all a single word uttered in a child's high-pitched scream.

'FLISSY!'

And I turned, and there before me was Alexander and he was looking at me. My foot slipped and I fell to my knees. I sprawled there, trying to make sense of it. He was looking at me, really looking at me. His eyes were on mine. He could see me. It seemed an eternity as we stood there, all of us turned towards the boy then the lightning flashed again, the thunder rolled and the first drops of heavy rain began to fall and the spell was broken.

'Alexander,' I said in wonder.

There was another flash of lightning and Fergus gave a howl and streaked for cover. Alexander whirled round as the little brown body hurled itself towards shelter.

'No Fergus,' he cried, 'not the Keep,' and then he too was running, his feet flying along the bridge towards the Keep. I wrested myself from the arms that clutched at me and threw myself after them while behind me feet pounded on the cobbles of the bridge. Fergus had disappeared down some bolthole into the Keep. Alexander was at the door now wresting it open with both hands. I called to him but my voice was lost in another clap of thunder then I too was in the Keep and swinging back the barely-closed door to the cellar, stumbling down the steps in the darkness and Alexander's voice was saying,

'Oh Fergus, you silly dog, don't you know it's dangerous in here?'

He turned to me and in the moment before darkness closed in on us I saw his eyes alight with joy though he said quite calmly, 'I can see again, Flissy.'

Then the door to the cellar closed with a grating thud and the light was gone.

# 8

I groped my way towards him, too distracted by his new-found sight to give much thought to the bolting of the door.

'Alexander,' I breathed and as my own eyes grew accustomed to the dark I saw his shining up at me in the pale blue of his face.

'I can see, Flissy,' he said tremulously, 'or at least I would be able to if it weren't so dark in here.' And he burst into noisy tears.

I cradled him in my arms as the sobs racked his thin body, murmuring words of comfort to him while Fergus licked his face and hands anxiously with his rough tongue. I let him cry, for they were healthy tears, and gradually the sobs began to subside and he rubbed at his eyes with his small fists. He looked down at the dog and said quietly.

'He's a beauty, isn't he Flissy?' And I could not speak for the lump in my throat as I realised that this was his first sight of Fergus. I nodded wordlessly and be began to speak again, his voice curiously matter-of-fact,

'I expect it was the shock. The doctors always said there was nothing wrong with my eyes.'

'Shock?' I repeated.

'Yes,' said Alexander calmly, 'she was going to kill you just as she killed my mother.'

My world rocked about me. 'But how did you know?'

'It was the words. She said those words once before, when we were in Italy, mother and I.'

And then it all came out. The trip to Italy, the picnic by the lakeside, the boy dabbling at the water's edge, then the voice clear as a bell in the mountain air saying those words; the boy turning, the flashing hooves and then darkness.

'What did they mean, Flissy?' he asked. 'I knew it was Italian and I knew it was bad, what she said, but what did they mean?'

His voice was earnest.

'They meant 'You must die',' I said quietly, and marvelled to myself how words spoken in a foreign language a year ago could by their repetition have such an effect.

He nodded again. 'Yes, I think I always knew deep down it was something evil.'

'You have always known?' I asked.

188

'I thought I must be wrong. Everyone said it was a terrible accident and then everyone said she was my mother.'

He clutched at me. 'But she didn't sound like my mother, Flissy, she didn't feel like her and I thought it was something to do with being blind.'

I hugged him, the poor confused child. 'And now?' I said.

'Now I don't mind so much. It was much worse when I thought she might be my mother. But she is wicked, isn't she Flissy?'

I smiled gently at his use of the word.

'Yes,' I agreed. 'She is wicked.'

The wicked queen in the fairy-tale, I thought.

'But now we've got to get out of here, Alexander,' I said.

I had not noticed before that my skirts were wet and that water was seeping through my shoes where I crouched. Dully the sound of thunder came to us and the urgency of our position was brought home to me. I kept my voice calm.

'Alexander, I am going to see if the door is truly barred as I fear it is. Wait here.'

I stumbled and groped my way towards the steps but I need not have bothered. The heavy wooden door was firmly bolted. It was so dark I could hardly see my hand in front of my face as I stumbled back, almost tripping over Alexander as I came.

'Are we trapped?' he said, a tinge of fear colouring his voice.

I was brisk.

'Not at all,' I said, 'someone will be along any moment to let us out.'

But the words masked my own fear, for I knew that no one knew we were here, no one but Carla. But surely we only had to wait?

'Come,' I said, 'we'll sit on the steps. At least it's dry there.'

We sat on the steps and I began to tell him a story and even then the full danger of our situation did not strike me until I felt the water lap at my toes. I put my hand to my feet and panic swept over me as I realised how quickly the level of the water had risen. The beaten earth floor must now be saturated, the water unable to drain away. Small pieces of hardened earth and deadwood bumped against my hand, and as I heard faint squeaking noises I realised that the rats would also be looking for higher ground and drew my hand back quickly.

'What is it?' said Alexander.

'Let's move up to the top of the steps,' I said briskly, 'then when we hear someone coming we can beat on the door to let them know we're here.'

We sat down, our backs against the solid wooden door and I wondered how much time we had and if the rain had stopped, then my hopes were dashed as I heard a dull rumble and the door behind me trembled at the blast while from far away came a faint insistent drumming sound — the rain. The vision of the culvert rose unbidden before my eyes, choked with dead leaves and twigs and the silt that the river had thrown up in its turbulent wake, and I saw the moat swell until it crept above the level of its retaining banks and the water that flowed steadily into the cellar became a torrent. I pushed the thought from me. We would still be safe here on the top step. Here we were at ground level. We would still be safe even if we did have to share our small sanctuary with the rats. I shuddered and pulled the boy closer to me while Fergus growled low in his throat, as if he too knew the rats would soon come. I thought I could make out some grey moving shapes in the darkness a little below us and was that scratching I heard? But imagination is a powerful thing and I thrust the thoughts from my mind. We will be safe I repeated to myself, then a clap of thunder seemed to fill my ears and I felt the whole tower shake. At first I thought it was the wind I heard but then I realised that down here that was not possible. The groaning continued and I realised at last that it was the timbers that supported the floor above. The warnings came back to me. The Keep is unsafe. The foundations are rotten. The spring tides have rotted the timbers. I called to mind the plan of the cellar. Great beams rose from the floor supporting the struts that held the floor above. The weight of those three stories seemed to press down on me. How many stones? If one of those beams collapsed how much of the Keep would come down with it? I saw in my mind's eye the whole of that massive tower crumple and cave-in on itself, then I had no more time for thought for a great rending crash that was not thunder split the air and my eyes and mouth were filled with dirt and dust and water beat against my face. I drew a deep breath, expecting any moment to be engulfed by the flood but it did not happen and Alexander was shouting.

'Look, Flissy, look!'

I opened my eyes.

The whole of the far side of the tower had collapsed, mercifully outwards, and the rain was gusting against my cheeks and though the sky was dark it was almost too light after our enforced blackness. I sat motionless for a moment before I realised the full danger of our situation. Above us the ruins of the Keep tottered against a storm-tossed sky and as another clap of thunder rent the air the structure groaned and bits of debris crumbled from the walls. The lightning lit the scene in lurid glow and I looked stupidly at the swirling water below us, at the flotsam thrown down from the floors above. For a moment I felt a great sadness as I looked at the tapestries, the chairs, all the lovely things that had furnished the Keep; then slowly — as if in a dream — a great oak chest balanced drunkenly on the remains of the floor above, toppled gently from its place, and crashed to earth throwing up a great spray of water and breaking the spell that held me.

'Come on, Alexander!' I shouted and, grasping him with one hand and the dog with the other, I threw myself into the water below. My breath caught as the icy waters closed around me lapping at my throat and Fergus broke away. I hefted Alexander up with both my arms and made to follow the dog which was paddling with great good sense towards the fallen rubble of the far walls. My skirts hampered me and Alexander felt like lead in my arms as I thrust my body through the water. I gasped as it lapped my mouth, deeper in some places than in others, and once two bright evil eyes looked into mine and I almost lost my balance as the rat darted round me through the water.

Bits of furnishings floated past me, and once more I reeled as Vida's face looked up at me from the portrait swirling on the waters. But though I wanted to, I could not rescue it and willed myself to drag the child and myself to safety. At last my feet touched stone and I almost threw Alexander from me onto the rubble. He began to scramble upwards whilst I hauled myself after him, my skirts heavy with water and dragging at my feet.

Fergus was once more in Alexander's arms and, as I drew a deep breath of sweet rain-drenched air, I could have laughed aloud. The ground was merely inches deep in water up here and we picked our way round the Keep whilst the moat bubbled and swirled and spread itself wide. Quickly, looking neither to one side nor the other, I led the child to the front of the Keep. Not until we were on the other side of the moat, across the bridge, would we be truly safe. We rounded the ragged walls of the Keep and I felt Alexander shrink against me, for there on the bridge was Carla and holding her shoulders, shaking her like a dog would a rat, was Lachlan with murder in his eyes. I shouted something, anything, to stop him as he thrust her back against the parapet of the bridge whilst Charles tried to pull his arms away. He turned and gradually the dark fury left his face and his hands slipped from her throat and I was running, Alexander at my side, then we were both in his arms.

Charles gave a cry and we turned quickly to see the black figure of Carla rushing towards the Keep. The outer door swung drunkenly on its hinges, almost torn from its moorings by the wind and she was unbarring the door to the cellar. Then that door too swung open and the thunder rolled once more and in the lightning that followed she turned and looked straight at me, her face a twisted mass of hate and disbelief, then she turned once more to the door. For a moment her body with its black silk gown flapping in the wind was very still, then high above the wind came her scream,

'Vida!'

and she plunged through the door as the thunder began to roll in the heavens and the sky was split with searing light. The Tower shook and shivered, seeming to hang suspended against the broken sky before it cast itself towards earth in ruins.

I remember nothing more, for then I fainted.

# 9

I have a dim memory of being carried back to the house, of Lachlan shouting for maids and Araminta fluttering beside me; of Dorcas thrusting Lachlan forcibly out of my bedroom as she undressed me, of hot scented water and clean sweet smelling sheets and then oblivion took over once more. When I awoke however, startled out of sleep by dreams of cold enveloping water and bright evil eyes, it was Lachlan's arms that held me and soothed me until I ceased to shiver. I looked up at him, at the face so dark and strained.

'Alexander?' I whispered.

The darkness left his face for a moment and his eyes glowed with warmth.

'Fit as a flea,' he said brusquely. 'Amazing powers of recovery, that boy.'

I hesitated. I was so lately woken from sleep that I began to wonder if it had all been a dream.

'His eyes,' I said tentatively.

Lachlan bent towards me and his hand touched my cheek lightly.

'Oh, my dear, what a great deal I have to thank you for.'

'Then it's true?' I said. 'I didn't dream it?'

'You didn't dream it,' he said.

I sighed and lay back on my pillows and to my horror I felt the tears slide from between my lashes.

'You're crying,' he said.

I sniffed miserably and dashed the tears away. 'I'm so happy,' I said inadequately.

His laughter rocked the bed where he sat.

'Perverse creature,' he said, but now other memories were returning.

'Carla,' I said.

His face grew sombre once more.

'Dead,' he said shortly. 'Killed instantly.'

'But why did she do it?' I asked. 'I heard her scream 'Vida' and throw herself into the Keep.'

He shrugged.

'Who can tell?' he said. 'Her mind was completely unhinged by that time.'

I thought of her in her last moments. Perhaps in the lightning she had caught sight of the portrait but what was the use of speculation. He was right. Best to forget.

'Alexander told me,' he was saying, 'about the accident and the words that brought his sight back. Perhaps in time I shall accept it as calmly as he does.'

I put my hand to his lips, smoothing out the lines of pain.

'Oh my dear, he has known for a long time and what he couldn't accept was denied by his body. Children are resilient. In time it will not hurt so much.'

His eyes were on my face, willing me to look at him as he said, 'If you are with me . . . 's

But I could not look at him. Memory had returned in full now and I could see my stepfather's face, hear the venom of his words.

'Felicia,' Lachlan's voice was gentle, 'you will not refuse me, not after you have given me such hope?'

The tears pricked at my eyelids as I said barely above a whisper, 'My stepfather . . . the things he said . . . '

I was interrupted by a great roar from Lachlan.

'Him!' he thundered. 'I've dealt with him!'

At once I was in a panic.

'You didn't . . . oh you couldn't have . . . '

He actually laughed.

'Kill him?' he said. 'That little rat? He wasn't worth the trouble.'

'But all those things he said,' I protested.

'He tried to say them to me,' said Lachlan with a grin. 'Didn't get very far though before I kicked him out. Very satisfactory I admit.'

I looked at him in wonder. For years my stepfather had haunted me, and now by laughing at him Lachlan had dispelled all those years of fear.

'Still not learned to trust me, Felicia,' he said, apparently highly amused. 'In that case the best thing is to marry me straight away. You'll learn all the quicker.'

I said quite calmly, 'Yes, Lachlan, yes please.'

I thought my ribs would crack at the force of the hug that engulfed me, then a voice said from the door,

'Not interrupting, am I?' And Lachlan cursed under his breath whilst I giggled happily.

'Come in, Charles, do,' I said.

He was followed by Araminta, Douglas, Alison, Alexander and, lastly, Fergus who both hurled themselves on me.

'Quite recovered?' said Charles breezily and Lachlan muttered darkly again.

'Really, Charles,' said Araminta reprovingly, much to my surprise. 'You'd think she'd just been caught in a summer storm instead of being locked up and half-drowned. Don't take any notice of him, Felicia, he's not sensible at the moment. He's made a fortune.'

I looked at Charles in amazement. He tried to look less delighted than he obviously was.

'True,' he said, unable to resist it, 'and on the Stock Exchange too. The essence of respectability.'

Light began to dawn.

'That was the gamble you were talking about? The one that would set you up for life?'

He coughed deprecatingly.

'Not gambling, Felicia; speculating.'

I had a twinge of conscience as I thought about my suspicions concerning him and Araminta's diamond.

'The two are not entirely dissimilar,' I said primly.

'Now it's no use being damping,' he said, 'or trying to be governessy. It's impossible sitting up in bed in a nightgown as pretty as that — even for you.'

I laughed, then my mouth dropped open in surprise as he said,

'Besides, it's in the nature of a last fling. My future wife disapproves of both gambling and speculation.' And he turned and took Alison's hand in his.

'Both equally immoral,' said Alison, but her eyes were dancing.

'But speculation's so much more respectable isn't it?' teased Charles. 'And you'll keep me respectable, Alison. About the only one who could.'

I looked at Alison, and marvelled that I could have thought her in love with Lachlan.

The look she was giving Charles was anything but respectable. I should have something to say to Araminta. She in turn was looking at Lachlan and me.

'I suppose you two have fixed it up then?' she said.

Lachlan drew himself up whilst I suppressed a smile,

'If by 'fixed it up' you mean have I asked Felicia to become my wife and has she accepted, then yes,' he said grandly but his moment was spoiled by Alexander's whoop of delight as he jumped off the bed and ran jubilantly round the room with Fergus at his heels knocking over furniture. I regarded him tolerantly while even Lachlan smiled and Araminta stuck out her lower lip and pouted beautifully.

'Oh well, Douglas, I suppose that just leaves you and me,' she said, shooting him a wicked glance that made him colour to the roots of his hair while the rest of us said in chorus,

'Oh, Araminta!'

## THE END

www.ingramcontent.com/pod-product-compliance
Lightning Source LLC
Chambersburg PA
CBHW051135020726

47501CB00005B/1519